The Valerons - Double Ante

As ramrod over the Valeron cattle, Sketcher takes Reese Valeron's place on a trip to the yearly auction in Chicago with Shane and Jared Valeron. A simple drawing becomes the impetus that quickly involves Sketcher with several street urchins, a person called Mother and an unsolved murder.

Meanwhile, Wyatt goes to visit a friend in the small town of Solitary. What starts out as a genial trip ends up as a battle with a rancher and his sons that leaves him fighting for his life.

The call goes out to come to Wyatt's aid. Jared and Shane leave Sketcher to deal with buying and delivering the prize bulls to the Valeron ranch. Others from the Valeron ranch join the conflict, arriving in Solitary to wait for Jared.

The battle with the Strang ranch could pit thirty men against Jared and his handful of men, while Sketcher is risking his life dealing with crooked cops and the leader of a Chicago gang.

Covering bets on two fronts, the chances are slim everyone will get out alive!

The Valerons - Double Ante

Terrell L. Bowers

A Black Horse Western

ROBERT HALE

© Terrell L. Bowers 2019
First published in Great Britain 2019

ISBN 978-0-7198-3003-7

The Crowood Press
The Stable Block
Crowood Lane
Ramsbury
Marlborough
Wiltshire SN8 2HR

www.bhwesterns.com

Robert Hale is an imprint
of The Crowood Press

The right of Terrell L. Bowers to be identified as
author of this work has been asserted by him
in accordance with the Copyright, Designs and
Patents Act 1988

Typeset by
Derek Doyle & Associates, Shaw Heath
Printed and bound in Great Britain by
4Bind Ltd, Stevenage, SG1 2XT

CHAPTER ONE

The man rushed up from behind Pamela Hutchings and a strong hand grabbed hold of her arm. She cried out from surprise as she was yanked around to face her pursuer.

'What be ye doing 'round here, lassie!'

It was not a question, but a demand. Pamela, because of a chilly wind and the late hour, was wearing a cloak with a hood. The garment, along with the dark shadows, kept most of her face hidden from the man in a police uniform. A single glance was enough to make out the badge on his shirt, which hung somewhat sideways, due to a fair amount of extra weight around his middle. He appeared flushed and out of breath, panting harder than one might expect from the singular act of exertion to overtake her.

'I'm on my way home,' she told him softly. 'This is the shortest route to my lodging.'

He glanced around quickly. 'Is it alone you are, lassie?'

'Yes. It's only another two blocks to the rooming house.'

'What else have you been a peeking at in the past few

minutes?'

Pamela shook her head. 'Nothing! I haven't seen any-thing. There's almost no one on the street at this time of night.'

He put both hands on her upper arms and pulled her closer. 'Begorra! You look like a street scavenger to me! Where did you come from?'

She bridled at the title, but withheld all emotion in her reply. 'I'm not a beggar. I told you, I'm on my way home.'

' 'Tis soliciting on the streets,' he continued to bedevil her. 'Be that what you're up to?'

'Not at all,' she stated defensively. 'I've been looking for work in the city. The laundry where I used to work shut down several weeks ago. I need to find another job.'

He grunted. 'I don't care for the way you keep to the shadows. It's like you're sneaking around and spying on people.'

'I've no reason to spy on people,' she said with a degree of bravado. 'It's a long walk into the city and I'm getting home later than expected.'

'Fair enough, lassie.' He growled a warning, 'Jus' see to it, I don't catch you stealing nothing.'

'I'm not a thief!' she declared. 'Stealing is a sin.'

'Spying on people is something of a sin, too,' he said.

Pamela attempted to pull away from him. 'Can I go?'

The cop hesitated a moment. 'There be some bad sorts in this part of town. You carrying a weapon of any kind?'

'No. Of course not.'

'Dangerous business, prowling these streets after dark.' He pulled out a jackknife and stuck it in her hand. 'Here, take this.'

Pamela looked down at the instrument and regarded

the cop with an inquisitive look. 'Won't I get in trouble for carrying one of these?'

'Nothing illegal about it.' He uttered a knowing snort. 'And if you end up becoming a street scavenger, you might need it to defend yourself.'

To hurry the end of the confrontation, she wordlessly stuck the knife into her pocket.

'Be off with you!' the officer ordered. 'And don't you be peeking where you shouldn't!'

Pamela hurried down the street towards her private rented quarters. It had been another wasted day, going from place to place, asking for work. All she had to show for her efforts were sore feet and an aching body.

'One day closer to getting kicked out on to the streets!' she muttered.

The rooming house was dark except for a single lamp next to the door and the flicker of a candle or light that emanated from a couple of rooms with windows facing the street. Quickly up the stairs, Pamela pushed open the door to her cubicle. Not bothering to light one of her precious candles, she found her blankets in the dark. She took a moment to shake the top cover, wary of insects, mice, or a dreaded rat. Fortunately, they seemed to avoid her stuffy apartment – perhaps because she never left so much as a crumb of food lying around.

Changing into her nightclothes, she snuggled in between her two blankets and tried to relax. She closed her eyes, weary from a fruitless day of rejection and disappointment. Although bad dreams often made for a fitful night, the exhaustion of her body could not be ignored.

Thankfully, this was a dreamless night and she rose to

another day of searching for any kind of job offered. Tossing on her robe, she took her turn at the single wash closet to clean up as much as possible. Her dress had begun to fray from neglect and wear. The once blue fabric had faded to a near-white and was threadbare in places. If she didn't find work soon, she would be down to her only other dress and be unable to pay next month's rent. Facing the brutal cold and winds of a Chicago winter, she hated the idea of having to solicit on the streets for any chore or bit of work that would earn a few cents for food and shelter.

Pamela used the hood on her cloak to cover her head. There was no rain, but there was the chill of fall in the early morning air. With a steadfast determination, she started her journey towards a different part of the city. Chicago was spread out over a large area, so she would continue to visit all the eating and laundry establishments. Someone must need a dishwasher, waitress, or help to clean up after everyone had gone. If only she could. . . .

'Papers! Two cents for the latest news!' a boy cried, hawking the daily edition of the local newspaper. 'Read about the woman vagrant who killed a local tavern owner.'

He continued to wander along the street with his bag of newspapers slung over one arm. 'Read the news!' he announced again. 'Read about the cloaked phantom who robbed and killed a businessman.'

Although she was desperately clinging to what little money she had, Pamela pulled the hood over her head to conceal her face as she approached the boy. She held out two pennies and the youth handed her a copy without attempting eye contact. He stuck the coins in his pocket and continued on, shouting the latest news story. Pamela ducked into the next alley and scanned the paper.

Quickly reading the lead article about last night's murder, she felt her blood turn cold. It stated that a mysterious woman, who used a hood to hide her face, had been seen running from the body of Rufus Lannigan. The local business owner had been attacked less than a block from where the policeman grabbed her . . . and the victim was killed with a short-bladed knife.

Short-bladed knife!

The words caused Pamela's knees to go weak. The cop! He was flushed and out of breath; he had killed that businessman, a known member of a powerful crime family! It's why the policeman wanted to know what she had seen!

Hurrying back to her sleeping room, Pamela had to physically and mentally fight down a great swell of panic. What could she do? If arrested, she would be thrown in jail for years – possibly the rest of her life! Her word would mean nothing against that of a policeman. With a grim resolve to survive, Pamela began to pack her few things. She knew of a secluded hiding place, next door to the laundry where she had worked. She had stumbled upon it when helping a child to locate her missing kitten. The small feline had been drawn to the concealed den because it offered heat. A major drawback – it was located nearby, well within the boundary of both the crime boss and the killer policeman. However, with winter coming on, it was the only place she knew of where she might hide out and survive.

After several months throughout the spring and summer, working as the only lawman in the mining town of Gold

Gulch, in the Dakota territory, Wyatt turned in his badge. He decided to head home to the Valeron ranch for an extended visit. However, there was no hurry, and he found himself thinking how nice it would be to spend some time with a lady friend.

Wyatt never figured to marry, so he felt comfortable frequenting a gentleman's parlour on occasion. Unlike many of the customers who visited such places, he didn't care for a quick visit upstairs with a complete stranger. He often had a drink or two with a lady first, perhaps taking a turn around the room to music, using a dance and idle conversation as a way to get to know her. Many nights he would spend an hour or two with one girl or another and never take it any further. It wasn't that he didn't lack the natural urge to be with a woman, only that he preferred to form a kinship with a gal . . . before sharing intimacy with her.

Reflecting upon his cousin, Jared Valeron, the two of them had gone to a parlour or saloon together a few times, but Jared never took a girl upstairs. He had a strong moral streak concerning womanhood. It kept him from fully enjoying a girl's company unless he really took a shine to her. Given the circumstances in most parlours, that didn't happen often, as it was the job of such girls to separate a man from his money as quickly as possible. Such an approach kept most of the hostesses from being the kind of 'nice' girl who would have peaked Jared's interest.

As for Wyatt, he had found a special girl here or there – three actually. One in Denver, but she had married recently; one in Cheyenne, who would likely end her career the same way one of these days; and his overall favourite – a diminutive young lady who went by the name of Remmy and resided in the town of Solitary. The small Wyoming municipality served both a boisterous mining community and a couple of sizable ranches. Being considerably closer to the town of Valeron than Cheyenne or Denver, he visited there about once a month when he wasn't working.

This night, he arrived at Maxine's, where the girl worked, shortly after dark. Maxine's place was one of the two gentleman's parlours in Solitary. He stabled his horse, figuring to spend the night – either with Remmy or at the one rooming house in town.

Maxine saw him enter and glided (she never really walked – her gait was the most feminine imaginable) over to give him a hug. She then took him by the arm, pulled him over to a private corner of the room, and regarded him with a solemn gaze.

'It's well past time for you to be stopping by,' was her greeting. 'Haven't seen you all summer long.'

Always the gentleman, Wyatt removed his hat before speaking. 'You look stunning as usual,' he said. 'Hard to believe you're almost as old as my mother.'

She laughed. 'I should have nothing but grey hair and wrinkles, looking after my brood of girls.'

'It's a full-time job,' he concurred.

'About Remmy,' she got down to business. 'She isn't feeling well. It's nothing too severe, but she probably won't be working for a few days.'

'You know me, Maxine. I'd be happy to sit with her for a few minutes, take her a meal or something. I consider Remmy to be more of a friend than a paid companion for an hour or two.'

11

The woman lowered her eyes, trying to hide something. It was enough to prompt Wyatt to place his hand on her shoulder.

'Maxine?' he coaxed. 'What is it? What's happened?'

The woman uttered a sigh of resignation. 'It's the Strang boys. They were here for a wild party last night.' She raised her hands in a sign of frustration. 'What can I do, Wyatt? They control a good portion of money that comes into this town. We have no law here – only whatever rules the mine or ranch owners choose to enforce when it comes to governing the behaviour of their men.'

'One of them hurt her?' Wyatt was instantly concerned. 'How bad is it?'

'There's a few bruises, but . . .' Maxine assured him quickly, 'the black eye is going to take a few days to clear up.'

'Why would anyone hit Remmy?' he demanded to know. 'She's about as sweet as any girl I've ever met in her profession.'

'It's like I said, Wyatt. Hud and Aldo Strang were drunk and out of control. When Remmy refused to go upstairs with them, one of them hit her. My bouncer tried to calm them down, but the pair turned on him. They beat him to the floor, then kicked and stomped him so bad he died this morning. It's their way of having fun – tearing up a saloon or getting into a fight.'

'And Remmy?'

Her sorrowful look preceded her regretful reply. 'They took her upstairs against her will.' She threw her hands up in despair. 'What could I do? Poor Keith was unconscious and bleeding on the floor, and no one in town opposes anyone from the Strang ranch. When they left, I tended her as best I could . . . but Hud and Aldo are a couple of savage beasts.'

'Who only fight with the odds on their side,' Wyatt snapped. 'I know their kind.'

'They aren't usually so destructive and vicious,' Maxine offered a defence. 'Last night . . . well, last night was the worst they've ever been.'

'How many are there in the family?'

'Ed Strang has four sons: Jack and Carver are the two older boys – they don't ever cause any trouble. Can't say the same for Hud and Aldo.' She shrugged. 'They are always looking for someone to knock around. The two of them killed a gambler a few weeks back when he caught them cheating. Like I said, they are completely out of control sometimes.'

'I'd like to see Remmy,' he told her, careful to conceal his inner rage. Even so, he added: 'And maybe it's time for law and order to come to Solitary.'

'Wyatt, I know you have a reputation as a town tamer, but this isn't your usual town. The miners and cowboys are all we have. There is no railroad and we're not located on a main crossing to anywhere else. This is an isolated burg out in the middle of nowhere. I doubt even God knows it's here.'

'I'm here,' Wyatt said tightly. 'And I'm for believing God has always kept an eye on me. Otherwise, I'd have been dead a long time ago.'

'You need support to pin on a badge. No one in town is going to grant you any authority, not when it could mean the end of their business.'

'What about you?'

'If I were to support you taking over as town marshal,

I'd be broke in a month. The miners and cowboys don't want law and order – they want to do whatever they damn well please!'

Wyatt gave that some thought. He had tamed several towns over the last few years, but he always had support of the town elders. No lawman could succeed without the people being behind him. Yet something had to be done. A few men couldn't behave like animals just because no one was carrying a badge. Someone had to force a degree of civility upon them.

'Have you hired a new bouncer?'

Maxine's shoulders sagged. 'After Keith being killed, who is going to work for me?'

Wyatt took a deep breath and let it out slowly. 'How much does the job pay?'

CHAPTER TWO

Sketcher – whose real name was Sidney Grey – had a contradictory personality. He was as mellow as a calm morning, able to draw most anything with his black charcoal marker, so realistic it seemed to come to life. Yet he was the first man up every morning, rousting the cow punchers, wranglers and other ranch workers out of bed. He never asked a man to do a chore he wouldn't do, was quick of wit and one of the most learned men on the Valeron ranch.

Shane and he often went fishing together and Reese trusted him to get any task done that was given him. As Reese had acquired himself a wife, Sketcher took his place on the trip back east to buy some Hereford bulls. Locke Valeron, who oversaw everything the Valerons owned, had brought in a couple of Hereford bulls last year and was pleased by the breed's offspring. Along with his own observations, he had read about the European cattle and was convinced Herefords would be the beef of the future. Hearty, thick at the neck, shoulders and hind quarters, a bull might weigh fifteen hundred pounds. Most steers ran upwards to a thousand pounds, and that meant a higher price for every beef sold.

So Locke had picked Sketcher, along with Shane and Jared, to make the journey back east. It would be the first time one of the three senior brothers – Locke, Temple or Udal – hadn't made the arduous trip to Chicago. It would also be Shane's first trip. Jared had gone several times before, so he knew enough about the stockyards and procedures to buy and ship the bulls home.

Thinking back, Sketcher's kinship with the Valerons was closer than to his own parents. They and his three siblings were a blur in his memory. He had been twelve when they left him at a home for wayward and orphaned children. They had deemed him too sickly to make the journey westward to a new home and new lives. And, in retrospect, they had probably been right. The six weeks aboard ship on the trip to America had caused Sketcher a dreaded seasickness that had sapped him of what little weight and strength he had. He could barely stand under his own power when they arrived at the port.

In spite of their benevolent intentions, the Children's Aid Society in New York had to deal with more children than they could handle. The orphan and displaced children's home had been a nightmare – sixteen boys of various ages in a room filled with bunkbeds. There was barely enough food or clothing and nothing to do most of the time. After eighteen months, Sketcher had put on enough weight to be shoved on to a train going west with over a hundred other children. Each major city along the way had arranged a greeting committee, taking ten to fifteen wayward kids for placement. Some folks had sent requests for the age and sex of the kids wanted, so a few children who fit those qualifications were given to parents who had vowed to take them in. Others, like Sketcher, having much less chance of being selected, were lined up on the station platform so any interested people could look them over. Occasionally, someone would pick one of them. The familiar phrase, being *up for adoption* became a constant for Sketcher. A strong-looking youth of fourteen would be snatched up by anyone looking for a potential slave for the next few years, someone who would earn their keep. Still being slight of build and less comely than average, Sketcher found himself one of the last unclaimed youths aboard the train.

That final stop in Cheyenne had been fortuitous indeed, as Udal and Faye Valeron were in town. They had just seen to the disposition of their youngest son, Heath Valeron, who had been a victim of an Indian attack. The youth had been on a trip with two of his friends, hunting rabbits and sage hens, when a small war party had killed them all. The army had not known who the boys belonged to, so their bodies were transported to Cheyenne until they could be identified.

While arranging transport for their son's body, Faye saw Sketcher sitting on the ground drawing. He and three remaining children were still unclaimed. One look at his art work and she began to cry. Having overheard details about the coffins and the trio of dead boys, he had been sketching the boxes and the grief he saw in the faces of their loved ones.

From that day on, Sketcher had been taken into the Valeron household and raised alongside Faye and Udal's sons: Martin, Faro and Wyatt. He was several years younger than his foster brothers, but they never picked on him. Instead, he became good friends with all three boys and ended up working alongside his adopted cousins – Shane and Reese. In the ten years after his arrival, he had risen from a gangly kid to become Reese's assistant foreman at the Valeron ranch. Now a man of normal stature, he was respected for his hard work, his knowledge about cattle and the duties required to run the ranch.

The three men, he, Shane and Jared, arrived in the town of Valeron on horseback, from there to proceed via the stage to Cheyenne. Then they would travel by train on the long trip to Chicago. The stage was running late so Jared went to visit with his brother, Brett Valeron – an ex-US Marshal and acting town sheriff – while Shane and Sketcher stopped by the Valeron accounting and book-keeping firm, run by Wendy Valeron and her betrothed, July Colby.

After Wendy and July had announced their engagement, Sketcher had outlined a vignette of the young couple and worked on it in his spare time. Once greetings were exchanged, he presented the piece of artwork to Wendy. The drawing had been fitted into a 12 × 15in decorated frame.

'It's beautiful!' Wendy exclaimed, whirling about to show it to July.

He bobbed his head in agreement. 'Son,' he said to Sketcher, 'you missed your calling. You ought to paint portraits for a living. I never looked that good in my entire life.'

Sketcher grinned shyly, a man keenly aware of his talent, yet uncomfortable with compliments. 'I tried to catch the you that Wendy sees when she looks at you, July,' he quipped, 'not the lame, ex-miner, washed-out cowboy the rest of us see.'

Wendy and July laughed.

'The two of you set a date yet?' Shane asked. 'Ma said Wanetta is going crazy with the planning already.'

'Mom has been nagging me, too,' Wendy answered. 'But we wanted a few months of working together first. I've still got a few things to learn from Martin, and July has to wade through all of the terms state or federal attorneys use when they write up their tax bills. Since we started up the firm, we've added a dozen or so new clients. Some days we are too busy to stop and eat.'

Shane said: 'I imagine you get to see quite a bit of Brett and Desiree, along with their new little boy.'

'I, and sometimes July, have a meal or two with them each week – either at their house or the local eatery. My little apartment upstairs doesn't have much room for entertaining.'

'And I bunk at Beulah's Boarding House,' July pitched in. 'I get two meals a day with my rent, so I don't spend a lot of money eating at a café.'

The four of them talked a while longer before Jared arrived. He hugged his sister and shook hands with July. He hadn't seen them in over a month.

'I can't believe Father is going to send you to the auction as the man in charge,' Wendy teased her older brother. 'Reese . . . yes; Brett . . . no problem; Martin, or even Troy or Faro; but you?'

'It's only to buy a few head of Hereford bulls,' Jared reminded her. 'I won't even be carrying a gun on the streets of Chicago. How much trouble can I get into?'

Wendy shook her head. 'Jer, you always find a way. You're like a magnet for trouble. You don't have to look

19

for it, it's always following you around.'

'We'll be there to watch over him,' Shane promised.

That caused Jared's sister to laugh. 'That's like throwing a saddle on a bucking bronc and telling the saddle it's the one in charge. You do whatever and go wherever Jer tells you.' Then she turned to Sketch, 'And you are going to be like a city kid tossed up onto the back of that same bucking bronc!'

'Regardless of what you think of my skills as a leader,' Jared defended himself with an air of superiority, 'I've yet to get anyone in the family killed. That ought to be in my favour.'

Wendy issued a snappy repartee: 'Just see that when we next get together you can still make the same boast.'

'Maybe you'd like to come along?' Jared kidded. 'You've never seen a stockyard like the one in Chicago. And they've got hotels and buildings that are ten storeys high.'

'I've no ambition to spend days travelling by train, thank you,' Wendy replied. 'The infrequent trips to Denver have been more than enough to crush what enthusiasm I had for riding on a train.'

'Might get to ride on one of them Pullmans if we get far enough east. Some people claim they are a palace on wheels.'

'I have all the comforts right here, Jer. And I don't have to travel a thousand miles.'

'Uh-oh, there's the stage!' Shane said, pointing out the window. 'With it running, late, they're gonna be in a hurry to get started back. We'd better grab our stuff and get ready to board.'

The five of them exchanged farewells and the trio left

the office with Wendy and July both wishing them good luck.

Pamela Hutchings knelt down to examine the bruise on Monte's face. There was swelling next to his eye, but the blow hadn't broken the skin.

'And this was Jigger's doing?'

'Him and a couple others.'

'Them bigger kids are getting meaner,' Tess said, the fear evident in her voice. 'Told us to stop selling on their street or they'd break some bones next time.'

Pamela pulled both of the children into her arms and hugged them. The pair were both about eight years old, her two best *gatherers* . . . as she called them.

'Maybe we ought to move?' Tess continued to worry. 'What if they come looking for us?'

'No one comes down here,' Pamela assured them. 'We're safe as long as you always make sure no one follows you.'

'We take the long way,' Monte assured her. 'That way we can look around good before we go through the sewer pipe.'

She looked them over. 'Did they take your matches?'

'Monte lowered his head and Tess shrugged. 'Them boys was too big to outrun. They even took the twelve cents we had earned.'

Pamela caressed their cheeks with a delicate hand. 'It's all right. We have more matches to sell.' Then she led them over to their makeshift table – two boards set between a drainpipe and the foundation. The cracked serving platter, which they had scrounged from a nearby hotel's trash, had several small sandwiches – crackers with

21

a slice of cheese – and a few very ripe orange chunks.

'Have something to eat and then try to avoid the Irish district. We need to earn enough to buy a loaf of bread and a can of condensed milk. We just have to get by another day or two and the stockyard sale begins.'

'You told us the selling was great last year!' Monte said, his mouth full of crackers.

'Yes, those cattle and hog buyers are usually quite generous. We earned enough money last year that it kept us through the worst of winter. Molly averaged more than a dollar on good days.'

Tess frowned. 'Ceptin' Molly ain't here no more.'

Pamela sobered at the memory. 'After she caught that cold, I was afraid it would turn into pneumonia. I had to take her to the hospital.' She sighed. 'Unfortunately, they cared for her until she was well, then turned her over to the children's society.'

'Now she's gone,' Monte said.

'Yes, those people stuck her on the train with a lot of other children and sent them all down the tracks. There was nothing I could do.'

'I miss her,' Tess said, her little face showing pain over the loss. 'When I come here, she was like my big sister.'

'She was the first child I took in,' Pamela said. 'I miss her, too.'

The sound of footsteps turned their heads. David and his younger sister had come through the tunnel. A bright smile shone on David's face.

'Annie made a friend,' he said about his four-year-old sibling. 'Some old lady gave her a quarter for one of her flowers. Then she give us these!' And he held out two sugar sticks.

'Wow!' Monte exclaimed happily. 'Way to go, Annie!'

Pamela took the money they had gathered and carefully broke the sugar sticks into equal-sized pieces for all four children. As the kids laughed and ate, she put away the money and made a careful inspection of the tunnel.

How long can I do this? She wondered. And to what end?

Three years had passed since her parents had died in a fire, leaving her alone and penniless. Her salvation had been the laundry, eking out a meager existence. Then things had gone from bad to worse. The laundry shut down and a murderous cop had blamed her for the death of a local businessman. For the past year, she had worked at nothing jobs, usually only a few hours or a day or two at a time, hiding out like an animal. A reward had been offered up by the cousin of the slain man, one of the big bosses on this side of town. She might have tried to contact someone high up in the police department for help, but the corruption in law enforcement had been exposed at most every level over the past few years. She couldn't trust anyone enough to speak up. To make such an attempt might land her in prison, facing a long sentence . . . or even death.

During her time in hiding, she had recruited and protected a number of young and vulnerable children who had been abandoned to the streets. She was called Mother, because she took on the role of provider and care-giver to her wards. But it was not a life, merely a test of survival. Eleven children had come and gone, most of them eventually accepting their fate with one of the overcrowded, overburdened children's aid or help organizations. But surrender was a gamble. Few of the kids were adopted locally. Most of them ended up stuck in an institution like criminals or placed on a train bound for the unknown. Stories about being sold into bondage, having to be separated from your siblings, then ending up as slave labour in factories or field workers; it was something many kids didn't want to face.

Counting the money the children had collected, she allowed herself a sigh of relief. There was enough for the bread and milk. If the kids could scrounge a little more, she could maybe get an apple or other fruit or vegetable. She knew, to be healthy, the kids needed more than bread and crackers.

A glance at the table warmed her heart and renewed her resolve. Four smiling faces, the laughter of children ... it had been so long since the children had been happy.

'Dear God,' she breathed the words softly. 'Please give me the strength to protect these darling children. I so want for them to have a chance at life.' Then as an afterthought, 'And thank you for the generosity of that dear woman. Amen.'

Remmy blinked against the light of day and discovered Wyatt Valeron sitting next to her bed. The window had a lace curtain and the walls had been coated with Sherman-Williams paint . . . pink with white borders. The night table was next to her bed, and she was snuggled under a floral-pattern bedspread. This was her private bedchamber, not a room for entertaining guests. As for the young woman, her long, raven-black hair partially covered one of her cloudy blue eyes – the one currently swollen shut. Her lower lip was twice its normal size and there was a dark mark where it had been split by a cruel set of knuckles.

'Please!' the girl pleaded through her puffy lips. 'Please, Wyatt! I don't want you to see me like this!'

But Wyatt reached out and took her hand between his own. He was unable to hide the mixture of pain and anger that raged through him like the heat from a blast furnace. It took a moment to unclench his jaw enough to speak.

'There, there, Remmy,' he whispered softly. 'It's going to be all right. It will take a few days, but the swelling will go down and the bruises will heal. Looking at you, I still see the charming girl I've grown to know these past few months.'

His gentle words prompted a lessening of the girl's misery. She couldn't smile, but she blinked with her good eye to remove the moisture.

'Gads,' she murmured. 'I feel so ugly right now.'

'I've looked the same way a time or two,' Wyatt volunteered. 'Only I didn't have your beautiful head of hair to hide the bruises.'

Remmy grunted. 'You make me laugh and I'll do a dance on your face. You won't be so funny when you are lying next to me looking like a pumpkin that fell off a produce cart.'

'See? That's not a problem – I favour pumpkin pie at Christmas dinner.'

'Thanks,' she said dryly. 'But if you start calling me *pumpkin*, I'll swat you a good one. I'm not real wild about the comparison.'

Wyatt turned serious. 'Why did the Strang boys do this to you?'

'It doesn't matter, Wyatt. I'll be OK. It might take a few days, but. . . .'

'Did both of them hit you or just one?' Wyatt asked again.

'There's nothing you can do,' Remmy avoided answering the question. 'You can't go up against the Strang family – they are too big, too powerful.'

'The Valeron spread isn't exactly a two-bit operation,' he replied. 'And don't worry about me. I'm not going to take on the whole bunch of them at one time.'

She rolled her head slightly in a negative gesture. 'That's one of the problems with that family. You can't go after one without them all joining in. They are a pack of coyotes; they gang up on their prey. Did Maxine tell you about Keith?'

'The bouncer?' Wyatt clarified. 'Yes.'

'He attempted to stop Hud when he hit me. Alto attacked him from behind and the two of them beat and kicked him until he was unconscious.'

'She told me about it.'

'Is he all right?' she asked. 'I mean, the Strangs were like wild savages.'

'I'm sorry, Remmy,' Wyatt told her gently. 'He died from the beating.'

Tears slid down her cheeks. 'He was . . .' she sniffed to stem the weeping. 'He was trying to protect me, to stop those two filthy creatures from. . . .'

When she couldn't continue, Wyatt patted her lightly on the shoulder. 'It's going to be all right. And I promise you, those vicious maggots will never hurt you again.'

Remmy started to sit up, but groaned in pain and sagged back onto the bed.

Wyatt pulled back the top blanket and saw the girl's torso had been wrapped with a thick bandage. 'They hit you in the ribs, too?'

'That happened when one of them pushed me against the bedpost. It knocked the wind out of me.' She hurried to explain, 'Maxine said it probably cracked a couple of ribs, but nothing seems to be broken.'

Wyatt gritted his teeth hard enough that it caused his entire jaw to ache. What kind of animals were these men that they could hurt such a sweet girl?

'Can you at least tell me what set these guys off? Was it something you said? Did you laugh at or insult one of them?'

'They got drunker than usual and became more rowdy. I refused to go upstairs with them and they became violent.'

'Hard liquor is no excuse. It's never an acceptable excuse!'

Remmy closed her good eye and lay back on her pillow. 'I don't really feel up to talking, Wyatt. If you don't mind, I'd like to try and get some sleep.'

'Go ahead and rest,' he said quietly. 'I'll just sit here with you for a few minutes . . . if that's all right.'

'You're the best, Wyatt,' she murmured. 'You always have been.'

CHAPTER THREE

Shane and Jared had decided to check out some of the night life – namely a casino and saloon a short way from the hotel. Sketcher took his art supply bag, which he always kept handy, and strapped it over his shoulder. It held his sketch pad and several sticks of charcoal and graphite, along with ordinary pencils and some clean cloths for wipes. He kept vigil for special people, places or things, always ready to stop and use his natural gift to project them onto his canvas.

After walking for a bit, he buttoned his jacket to ward off the cooler late afternoon air. The light would soon fade, but Sketcher hadn't seen anything to motivate him to put it to paper. As he wandered back towards the hotel, he spied a little girl – no more than four or five years of age. She was bundled in a worn little coat and had a shawl wrapped over her head and around her shoulders. The garment appeared longer than she was tall.

'Wanna buy sum matches?' she asked timidly, when she caught him looking her direction.

'My, but you're out late,' Sketcher told her, squatting down to speak to her. 'It's getting dark. Shouldn't you be getting home?'

'I need to sell sum more matches,' she said in a sweet little voice. 'Won't you buy one?'

Sketcher searched the street and walks, but the little tyke seemed to be alone. When he gave her a second look, he was struck by her adorable innocence.

'How much for the matches?' he asked.

'A penny each,' her presentation was automatic. 'Or get three of 'um for two cents.'

'Tell you what, sweetheart,' he said in a kindly voice. 'If you will pose for me — let's say for five minutes — I'll give you a dollar.'

The child gasped and her eyes grew wide. 'A whole dollar?'

'Yep.'

'What do I gotta do?'

'Just pose for me long enough that I can put your image on a piece of paper.'

A petite frown came into her face. 'What's pose mean?'

He pointed to a wall that would make a good back-drop. 'You only have to stand in front of the building and let me draw a picture of you. It will only take a couple minutes.'

'And for that I get a dollar?'

'That's right.'

The girl hurried over to the structure and turned around to face him. He asked her to not smile, but rather to look back at him and relax. 'And try not to move,' he added to the instructions.

Sketcher worked quickly, starting with the outline of her face and adding in the scarf and a rough draft of her clothing. As he began to work on her eyes a shadow fell over his drawling pad.

'What's going on, mate?' a gruff voice demanded to know. 'We gotta law against vagrants.'

Sketcher glanced at the man. He was in a police uniform and displayed all the warmth of a bulldog about to bite.

'There's no vagrant here, officer.' Sketcher responded politely. 'I've hired this young lady to model for me. I'll see to it she gets home all right.'

'I've seen you before,' the cop snarled at the child. 'You be one of Mother's nits.'

The girl tried to dart away, but the man was too quick. He grabbed her by the arm to prevent her escape.'

'What's the problem, officer?' Sketcher wanted to know. 'You are ruining my sketch.'

'Best get along,' the big man ordered, lifting the child up to hold her in one arm. 'This here be no concern of yours.'

Sketcher flipped the page on his art pad. 'Hold that pose for me, would you?'

The cop scowled. 'Do what?'

Sketcher began to outline the man's features. 'It will only take a moment.'

The man craned his neck trying to see. 'What are you doing?'

'I'm making a sketch of you,' he replied easily. 'That way, when I go to the local police station to file a complaint about you harassing one of us out-of-town cattle buyers, the captain or whomever is in charge will know who to discipline.'

The man took a backward step. ' 'Tis a cattle buyer you be?'

Sketcher continued to work on the drawing while he explained he was in Chicago with a couple others to buy several prize bulls for the ranch in Wyoming. Then he paused from his sketching. 'Correct me if I'm wrong, but doesn't the local government get a generous portion of income from the taxes derived from the money we stockmen spend in your fair city – not to mention the sale of livestock?' Sketcher sniffed impudently, hurrying to finish the man's likeness. 'I believe your discourtesy to one of we prospective buyers will garner you a severe reprimand.'

The man's face worked as his brain tried to sort out what he'd been told. He glanced at Sketcher's work and suffered a jolt.

'Hey! That's me!'

'Nothing art-worthy, but I believe your superiors will recognize my crude representation.'

Without warning, the policeman practically threw the tiny tot into Sketcher's arms, forcing him to drop his drawing material.

'Move along, Mate!' he growled. 'Don't be here when I come back.'

Sketcher watched him amble down the walk, then looked down at the little girl. She was staring right back at him, her eyes wide in amazement.

'I better get you home,' he said.

'What about the dollar?' she asked, having not forgotten his promise.

Sketcher bent down and picked up his materials. He kept the girl on one hip, while he slipped the things back into his bag on the other side.

'We'll complete our deal when I get you home. Which way is it?'

Ed looked up as his eldest son entered the sitting room. He lifted a bottle of beer in greeting. 'There's another one on the table. Ain't real cold, but it does cut the dust from your throat.'

Jack ignored the offer. 'I was in town today, picking up that load of wire for the holding pens.'

'Need some help unloading?'

'Carver is handling it. I told him to make Aldo and Hud lend a hand.'

Ed grunted. 'Good luck getting the boys to do any work. We've been trying for years to get them to pull their weight.' He sighed. 'I blame your ma. She always let them slide by without doing any chores, while you and Carver were out working alongside me.'

'Well, you'll be proud of your two youngest boys,' Jack said. 'They beat up one of Maxine's girls last night and pounded and kicked the bouncer so badly, he died a few hours later.'

'High strung,' Ed excused their behaviour without a degree of censure. 'I was on the wild side until I married your ma.'

Jack put his hands on his hips. 'This isn't being high strung, Pa, it's damned cruel and stupid! People are soon going to tire of watching those morons commit murder!'

Ed glowered at Jack. 'What's the big deal? So they knocked around one of the whores and showed the bouncer who is the boss of the valley . . . so what?'

'The girl was Remmy. You know the one. She's special. She only goes upstairs with a few select men. She isn't the same as the others.'

Ed sneered: 'Serves her right, thinking she's too good for my boys.'

Jack swore. 'Doesn't anything those two do ever put a dent in your thick hide? They beat up the nicest girl at the parlour; they killed the bouncer; and a few weeks back they killed that gambler in cold blood. What line do they have to cross before you put your foot down?'

'They're just blowing off a little steam, son. Don't take it to heart.'

'Well, you best be having a talk with those spoiled brats, or one or both of them is going to end up lying in a pine box.'

'What are you talking about?'

'A gun slick arrived in town, one who was very fond of Remmy. He ain't one bit happy about what Hud and Aldo did.'

Ed allowed a smirk to cross his face. 'Ain't no gunman gonna take on the Strang family. You're getting worked up for nothing.'

Jack remained with his hands still on his hips, showing his frustration. 'You make excuses for them, but one day Hud and Aldo are going to kill someone who matters. I, for one, am not going to lift one finger to keep them both from ending up in jail.'

The statement caused Ed to scowl. 'You'll do what I tell you to do, boy! I'm your father, and what I say is what we do!'

'No, Pa,' Jack did not back down. 'I'm telling you, it's time to rein in Hud and Aldo. Rein them in before it's too late.'

The old man fixed a hard stare on his eldest son, but Jack didn't flinch. He had become a man, reliable, steady, and with a mind of his own. Ed couldn't fault Jack for being the man he had always wanted him to be.

'All right, Jack,' he finally gave in. 'It sounds like the boys are getting carried away with their fun. I'll speak to them and tell them to behave. That suit you?'

'Yeah, Pa,' Jack replied, ultimately softening his stance. 'That suits me fine.'

Wyatt was on the dark street to meet the two men as they arrived by stage. Tiny stepped down and the coach rose a couple of inches. So called Tiny, from the time he was eight and weighed over a hundred pounds, the man was jovial and had an infectious laugh. Not a bad-looking sort, Tiny was built like a bullet, heavy about the chest and shoulders, yet he handled his 250 pounds without being bulky or awkward in his movements. Around the Valeron ranch, he was able to bulldog a nearly grown steer and out-wrestle any man on the place. He was formidable because of his agility, combined with his muscular arms and vice-like grip.

As for Doggie, he was quiet, almost taciturn most of the time. He enjoyed being around the other guys and joining in when there was fun to be had, but he had a reserve that hid his thoughts or opinions. The one thing Doggie possessed, he was wholly dependable and never walked away from a chore. Having been with the Valerons for seven years, he was one of several hands who was invited to the main house for Christmas dinner and most of the other family functions.

Wyatt shook hands with both men and announced, 'They said the stage sometimes didn't get here until midnight. You made good time.'

'Good weather all the way,' the driver reciprocated from his place on the coach seat. 'Besides which, I wanted a decent night's sleep before heading out in the morning.'

Wyatt gave him a wave, then turned to the two men from the family ranch. 'I'm glad to see you boys. I wasn't sure if I should expect you tonight or tomorrow.'

'That don't sound good,' Tiny responded to the greeting. 'If you need our help, it must be something so lowdown, dirty, or dangerous that none of your kin would agree to it.'

Wyatt laughed. 'Actually, I would have summoned Jared, but he is back east, in Chicago buying some bulls for breeding.'

Tiny elbowed Doggie. 'See what I told you? Wyatt's gonna make us his deputies or some such thing.'

Doggie grinned. 'Always wondered how it felt to pack a badge.'

'You're a fair hand with a gun,' Wyatt spoke to him, 'but I'm hoping to avoid a war.'

'So why did you wire Mr Valeron and ask for us to join you?' Tiny wanted to know.

'First off, grab your things and I'll get you settled in. Maxine owns the vacant trading post at the edge of town. She's offered it to us for free.'

'You mean that rundown shanty we passed up the street?' Tiny yelped. 'Free is too durned expensive for staying there.'

Wyatt laughed. 'It isn't so bad. It has three rooms, a water pump and outhouse. You two can spruce it up a little during your spare time. Shouldn't need it for more than a coupla weeks.'

Tiny gave a doubtful look at Doggie. The other man shrugged.

'Is it too late to get a ticket for back home?' Tiny joked.

'Boys, I've got the best job in town lined up for us. Trust me.'

'Whatta' you think, Dog?' Tiny asked his friend.

'Wyatt ain't never lied to us.'

'OK,' Tiny agreed. 'We'll gather up our gear and you can show us our new bunkhouse.' Then he frowned. 'What about you? Where are you staying?'

'Maxine's parlour. I have a room out back.'

'See that, Dog?' Tiny complained. 'He gets to bed down under the same roof with a bunch of beautiful gals – we get a run-down trading post full of mice and bedbugs.'

'Same treatment as always,' Doggie stated in a monotone voice.

Once the two had picked up their belongings, the three of them walked along the street. They passed by a saloon, a cafe – which both had lights on – and the town's only general store, which was dark and closed for the night. Within sight were another building or two, a barber shop/bath establishment, a hardware store and a bakery . . . all of them dark and shut down for the night.

'Place has all the comforts,' Tiny spoke up. 'Don't see any jail or bank.'

'The saloons have their own security. The stores keep most of their money in the King High saloon and casino. They pay a modest fee to stash their valuables; it's the biggest, most secure place in town.'

The inside of the old trading post had one table with a bench on either side. There was a small bedroom, having been for the lone man who ran the place. It was dusty, dank and stuffy inside. Once Wyatt lit a lamp, it illuminated the only window, so dirty it would have looked dark in the middle of the day.

'At least most of the shelving and racks have been stripped from the place,' Tiny muttered. 'We won't be cramped for room.'

'Probably burned everything for firewood before he went broke,' Wyatt said. 'The third room was for storage. Still has a couple of old Elk hides on the floor.'

'Bet there's a nest of bugs and mice living under it,' Tiny said. 'That single pot-belly stove is all I see for cooking and heat. Be a hard winter if we're still here when cold weather sets in.'

'I'm hoping it won't take that long to get this sorted out,' Wyatt told them with a wry grin. 'Once the few rowdies understand the new rules I'm putting in place!'

Sketcher had to bend so low he was practically crawling along the entrance way. It was a four-foot diameter old pipe that terminated at a run-off ditch that emptied into a sewer drain. He had to sidestep several bits of trash and a puddle or two of water. When the little girl reached a dead end, she pulled aside a thick piece of cardboard to reveal a hole in a rock foundation. Once through it, he discovered a fair-sized room, lit dimly by a single candle. He took note of a number of pipes running overhead and a few going through the floor of whatever was housed above. He could hear the hum of some kind of machinery, possibly the rumble of a huge boiler.

'Annie!' a woman's voice cried in alarm. 'What on earth?'

The little girl ran over to her excitedly. 'This man's gonna draw my picture, Mother! He says he will pay us a dollar!'

Sketcher was stunned. The young lady – maybe twenty years of age – was attired in a black dress and had donned a black cloak with an equally black hood. She had obviously been about to leave, probably to seek out the little muffin who was now at her feet. A quick look around revealed several beds on the ground along one wall and a crude table and two short benches out in another clearing. Three other children, none looking more than seven or eight, were watching intently, as if he was the first live man they had ever seen.

'I beg your pardon, ma'am.' Sketcher gave her an easy smile. 'I was attempting to do a sketch of the little tyke when a policeman showed up. He threatened to take her away as a vagrant.' He cocked his head in a helpless motion. 'I had no choice but to talk him out of it and bring her home.'

The young woman shrugged out of her overgarment and approached him. She did not readily make eye contact, as if uncomfortable at having to speak to a stranger. Stopping a step away, she was close enough for him to make out her features. He observed her hair was unkempt and the clothes were quite dirty – undoubtedly from living in an underground burrow. Even so, he deduced she was not altogether unattractive.

'The policeman mentioned you were this child's mother?' he queried, displaying puzzlement.

'No,' she answered softly. 'It's what my collection of wayward waifs call me . . . Mother. I protect and care for them. They have all been either orphaned or abandoned to the streets.'

'Say no more,' Sketcher told her. 'I came from the streets myself.' He shook his head and briefly explained his arrival in America and subsequent ending up at the Valeron ranch.

When finished, she said: 'Then you know first-hand how inadequate the children's aid societies are in these big cities.'

It was a statement, so he merely nodded his accord.

For a short span of time the young woman studied him. Though she and the children were all in need of a bath, the children's clothes were relatively clean. Mother's hair was quite long, and while in a degree of disarray, he deduced it to be a rich oak in colour, matching her sparkling brown eyes. Her lips were a cross between truculent and sensual, with a diminutive nose to match her fairy-shaped face. With dark eyebrows and dimpled cheeks, she could have been quite comely if ever prompted to smile. It was not her features, however, that allowed him to see her inner beauty, but her unmistakable compassion for others. Here was a woman who had withdrawn from society, yet she was looking after four children all by herself.

'Forgive my lack of courtesy,' she broke his steadfast perusal. 'Let me introduce you to my brood. Annie, you have met. She is four years old. Her big brother is David; he will be six next month. Tess and Monte are both eight years old . . . as near as either of them can remember. Annie and David's father was a widower and died of fever. Both Tess and Monte were turned out in the streets because their mothers could no longer care for them. They don't know what happened to their fathers.'

'It's a shame that there aren't more willing parents to take in these darling kids.'

The woman sighed, 'Yes, I can only do so much as I lost my job when the laundry closed down. Selling matches on the street for pennies isn't much of a life for the children.'

'Or you.'

She flashed a weary smile. 'They are worth the effort.'

'I must confess,' Sketcher was candid. 'You are something of a marvel ... Mother. To care for four small children is a task I would hesitate to undertake, and I have a home and a good job.'

She dismissed his praise. 'What's this about a drawing?'

Sketcher grinned. 'If you could manage another candle or two for light, it will take but a few moments to show you.'

The woman gave a nod of permission, then asked Monte to light some candles. Sketcher had Annie stand next to the wall and resume the pose she had been using before they were interrupted by the policemen. Three or four minutes later, he finished the sketch. He turned it around to show to Annie and the other three kids.

'Wow!' Monte exclaimed. 'It looks just like Annie!'

Mother came to appraise his effort and was also impressed. 'It's very accurate and lifelike. You are an exceptional artist,' she lauded his handiwork. 'What did you say you did to earn a living?'

Sketcher always carried a few copies of his work. He pulled them from his shoulder bag and held them out one at a time for the group to see. The sketches showed two men branding a calf, a running stallion with a dozen mares following, the chuck wagon at dinner time during a trail drive, and several other pictures that gave an overview of life on a cattle ranch.

'Of course, I only brought a few sketches with me,' he explained, tucking the drawings back into the satchel. 'The Valerons are a big family – three brothers and their wives and kids, totalling about a dozen, not including grandchildren. I'm something of an adopted child, treated like one of their kin.'

'A successful tale, considering you started out the same as my children.'

'About that,' Sketcher asked her. 'Why hide out in this den? Can't you get some help from one of the children's rescue organizations?'

She sighed her dejection. 'Their solution is to usually put them on a train going west. I am more than willing for them to take a child, providing they have suitable parents lined up, but. . . .' She gazed at him with an informed scrutiny. 'Well, you know the risks if they put you on the train.'

'Yes, I was placed up for adoption at five stops before the Valeron family took me in. I was very fortunate indeed.'

'You said you'd give me a dollar?' Annie reminded him, having walked over to tug on his pant-leg.

'And you have earned it,' Sketcher replied, smiling down at her. He dug out a silver dollar and put it in her small hand.

'Have you eaten?' Mother asked. 'We don't have much, but you are welcome to join us.'

'Only if you'll allow me to return the favour,' Sketcher replied. 'I'd like to take all five of you to a nearby cafe or eatery. What do you say?'

41

The lady physically withdrew at the idea. 'I . . . I don't go out except to buy supplies. My name is Pamela Hutchings and there is a warrant out for my arrest.'

'If it's for vagrancy, I believe, with my help, we can get that dismissed.'

'Um . . . no,' she said in a hushed tone of voice. 'It's for murder.'

CHAPTER FOUR

It was a sprawling yard, with a two-storey house, corrals, barn, tack-shed and bunkhouse. Wyatt rode up to the hitch rail out front and climbed down from his horse. Before he could tie off his mount, a young man opened the front door.

He looked to be in his early twenties, stocky-built, with dirty blond hair and yellow-brown eyes. Sucking in his gut to bolster the size of his chest, a haughty sneer took charge of his face.

'What's your business here, stranger?'

More of a demand than a question, Wyatt answered politely. 'I'd like a word with Edmund Strang. This is the Strang house isn't it?'

The impudent joker appraised Wyatt from head to foot, taking note of his cool demeanor and the Peacemaker Colt in a well-worn but painstakingly maintained holster. The weapon was tied down, but the riding thong was not looped over the trigger. It was ready for instant use.

He puffed up like an arrogant rooster. 'Pa didn't say he was expecting company today.'

'I'm not company,' Wyatt said easily. 'Tell him he has a guest.'

'A pushy sort, ain't you?' the kid retorted, as if ready to pick a fight.

'You must be the youngest pup in the Strang pack – Aldo. Is that right?'

'Mebbe . . . mebbe not.'

Wyatt shook his head. 'Sonny, if you aren't smart enough to know who you are, you'd best let me introduce myself to your pa.'

Before the kid could respond, a booming voice called from inside the house. 'What's all the yammering going on out there, Aldo?'

'A man to see you, Pa,' the boy called back.

'So open the damn door and let him in!' Ed commanded. 'We ain't got time for no foolishness. Your brothers will be wondering where we're at.'

Aldo backed to the doorway and jerked his thumb. 'Pa's inside.'

Wyatt went past Aldo and located a heavy-chested man sitting in a big lounge chair. Upholstered in expensive dyed-black leather, the chair had seen its best days, worn at the arm rests until the colour was a dingy grey. The man was busy tugging on his boots, but lifted his head to look at Wyatt, squinting through the strands of hair that fell over his eyes.

'State your business, stranger,' Ed Strang ordered. 'What do you want?'

'I'm here to collect for the damages your boys caused at Maxine's Parlour the other night.'

'Damages?'

Wyatt didn't bother to explain. 'It's a hundred

44

dollars . . .' he said. Then, before the old man could reply, he added: '. . . for you. Another two hundred each for your two sons! The total is five hundred dollars.'

Ed chuckled. 'So that's it? We got no laws, so you think you can come out here and demand money from me.'

'It's a new rule in town,' Wyatt explained. 'Anyone who injures a person or destroys property is to pay for the damages. If they refuse, they will be banned from entering that establishment.'

'Say what?'

'Five hundred dollars, Mr Strang.' Then he repeated the amounts: 'Two hundred for each of your sons involved, plus another hundred for you – seeing as how you didn't raise them to respect other people or their property.'

'I ain't gonna pay you a single dime!' Ed countered. 'But I can see to it that you leave my ranch draped over the back of your horse. How's that for a better offer?'

Wyatt had been careful to position himself with his back to a wall. He had a clear view of the room, the hallway to the rest of the house, and could also watch both Ed and Aldo.

'If you refuse to pay damages,' he went on calmly, ignoring Ed's threat, 'then you and your boys, and everyone else working or living on the Strang ranch, will not be welcome at Maxine's parlour.'

'Hell!' Aldo chortled inanely, 'that old bawd ain't even got a bouncer no more. We kicked the stuffing out of him and left him lying in his own blood.'

'Yes, you and your brother killed him.'

Rather than surprise or concern, the man snickered. 'Guess he wasn't as tough as he thought.'

45

'I reckon you and your brother suffer from the same notion,' Wyatt stated. 'Being as tough as you think, that is.'

Aldo stomped over to stand in front of Wyatt. The man was easily as big as Wyatt, built much like his father. He eyed Wyatt with open disdain, then spit on the floor at his feet.

'You thinking of taking us on?' He snickered his contempt. 'You don't look near as capable as that two-bit bouncer.'

Wyatt displayed a sympathetic mien. 'I suspect your eyesight is about on a par with your intelligence, sonny.'

The snide delivery of the statement provoked Aldo into action. He immediately launched a roundhouse swing that would have removed Wyatt's head from his shoulders.

Wyatt ducked under the blow, and in a swift, singular motion, side-stepped quickly and drew his gun. Before Aldo could recover from the force of his swing, Wyatt brought the gun upward in an arc and clouted the boy wickedly alongside the head. Aldo dropped to his hands and knees from the brunt of the gun barrel smacking his temple.

Ed started to come out of his chair, but Wyatt levelled the gun at his middle, cocked and ready to fire.

'I'd prefer to keep this civil,' Wyatt warned him. 'But make no mistake . . . I mean what I say. You can either pay the fine, or you and your boys, and every cowhand on your ranch is forbidden to enter Maxine's place.'

Ed glared at him, then looked at his semi-conscious son. 'There's a third choice I can make,' he threatened icily, rising slowly from his chair.

'If you're thinking about taking me on, it will be the last mistake of your life, Strang.' Wyatt holstered the gun as naturally as another might wipe his brow. 'You pay the fine, rein in your boys, and we'll have no trouble.' Then he fixed the man with a hard stare. 'But make no mistake, the very next time any of your family or hired hands hurts one of Maxine's girls, I'll put their carcass in the ground.'

'Meaning you'll kill them?'

'When I settle a dispute, I do it permanent.'

'You talk real big while wearing that gun on your hip,' Ed said, glancing down as his son began to stir. 'But knocking down my youngest with a dirty trick of a move don't mean you can take on Ed Strang. I've got a man or two on the place that are fair hands with a gun.'

'Trust me when I tell you, they won't want to go up against me.'

'Yeah? And why is that?'

'Because my name is Wyatt Valeron, and I'm Maxine's new bouncer.'

'Wyatt Valeron!' Ed declared, the shock visible in his make-up. 'You're Wyatt Valeron! And you're working for a house full of whores?'

Rather than reply to that, Wyatt returned to his original perspective. 'Five hundred dollars: a hundred for Maxine, two hundred for the bouncer's kin, and two hundred for the girl your boys beat up. Pay up, or every man-jack on your place is barred from entering Maxine's parlour.'

Ed sighed, more in resignation than defeat. 'All right, Valeron. I'd already decided to speak to the boys about not being so rough.'

'And the payment for damages?'

The man walked over to a cabinet that had a bottle of liquor sitting on it. He opened a drawer and removed several bills. There was no remorse in his expression. He was giving in, not giving up. He had grown used to pushing people around and allowing his boys to do as they pleased.

Wyatt accepted the payment without showing any sign of victory or relief. Both men understood the other. Wyatt had taken this hand, but the game was far from over.

'There's no law in Solitary,' Ed mentioned casually. 'You won't find any support if you try and tame the town.'

'I'm not hiring out for the community,' Wyatt replied. 'This is personal.'

Ed appeared satisfied with his response. Rather than make a threat, Ed lifted one hand and gave it a flick . . . like shooing a fly away from food on the table.

Wyatt offered neither a word nor gesture. He stuck the money into his pocket, rotated about and left the Strang home. The meeting had gone about as he had predicted, but only because the other three boys had not been home. Had he been facing all five. . . .

Sketcher made an excuse to part company with Jared and Shane for the second night in a row. After stopping at a store, he made his way to the hiding place with an armful of food. With the bread, fruit, and meat, Pamela prepared a regular feast for the six of them. He held back on removing the freshly baked pie from his bag until all of the plates were cleaned. Watching the children happily eat the dessert until they were stuffed was the most enjoyable thing he had done in his life.

After the meal, while the jubilant children were playing

together, Pamela related the fateful night when fire took her parents. She went on to cover the next three years working at a laundry. Lastly, she told how, once the laundry closed, she had been forced to pander for work on the streets and earn money where she could. When she discovered a wandering, unwanted child, she took her in . . . then another, and another. Soon she was organizing them into a sales force, designating areas for each and arming them with matches or flowers and sometimes apples – when they were available. Several children had stayed with her for a time, then decided to take their chances and surrendered to the child services groups.

She halted her history long enough to put the children to bed for the night. Pamela led them in their nightly prayers and kissed each of them goodnight. Instead of asking Sketcher to leave, she took the last burning candle and led him down a narrow tunnel between several pipes. The plumbing ran the width of the building and they finally stopped at a dead end wall. There was a single crate that had been placed on the dirt floor next to the union of an eight-inch pipe. There was a bit of a ledge from the rock and mortar foundation where she placed the candle. From the amount of wax, it appeared there had been many placed on the spot before. Obviously, the woman had spent many hours in this very spot.

'This pipe carries heated water to a washing room upstairs,' Pam explained. 'I believe there is a boiler on the other side of this partition. It's often the warmest place in this basement.'

Sketcher motioned to the crate. 'Sit down, won't you? I'll just hunker down against the wall.' She did so, folding her hands in her lap, and he turned serious.

'Now, what about this charge? You said it was for murder?'

Pam told him of the events of the night when she had been given the knife by the policeman. She was certain he had killed the man in question, because there was still blood residue on the blade.

'What can you tell me about this cop?' He dug out the outline of the policeman who had harassed him and Annie. 'Is this his likeness?'

'Yes, that's him,' she said. 'His name is Gruff McGowan. I learned from a few of the street kids about him. He and several others – some of them quite high up in law enforcement – are involved with the numerous criminal groups in this part of town.'

'And the man who was killed?'

'He was a cousin to one of the main gangs who run the saloons and parlours. One of the kids on the street told me McGowan was demanding more money for the protection and control of the streets. The two of them got into a fight and Rufus Lannigan ended up dead. Moments after McGowan's run-in with Lannigan, he grabbed me on the street. He gave me what I'm sure is the murder weapon, using the pretense that I should carry it for protection.'

'Then,' Sketcher postulated, 'McGowan tells everyone he saw you running away from the dead body and they put the blame on you.'

'Who is going to take the word of a street person over that of a policeman?'

Sketcher rubbed his chin, pondering options. 'I can see your situation is dire,' he admitted. 'And you claim there is a reward offered?'

'It's Big Mike's doing; he is the victim's cousin. He runs one of the gambling houses and several other businesses. I've seen his wife once or twice at the store, but I've never seen him or spoken to anyone in their family.'

'Anything else you know about him?'

'Only that his birthday is day after tomorrow. They've had a big celebration for him each year since I ended up in this part of town. The crowd he invites uses a whole city block and they have food, drink and dancing. The music usually lasts until midnight.'

'A birthday party, huh?' Sketcher suddenly had an idea. 'That could work to our advantage.'

Pamela pinched her eyebrows together in a puzzled frown. 'What do you mean – *our* advantage? None of this has anything to do with you.'

He grunted. 'We share a mutual bond, Miss Hutchings. I was a lost, unwanted boy, and you are a host mother to a bunch of unwanted kids. We both know what will happen to Annie, David, Tess and Monte if you are grabbed and thrown into prison. It will be the end of what little freedom they have. Next stop will be on one of those trains for orphans and abandoned children. If they are lucky, one of the four might end up in a decent home. The better chance is they will all end up working for a mistress or master, spending sixteen-hour days slaving at a mill or on a farm or plantation.' At her uncertain silence, he continued. 'I know what is waiting. I was there. I saw the people who took in the unwanted children.'

With an offhand gesture he admitted, 'True, there were a few who were sincere about offering an actual home to a child, but most of those had filed a request for a child. You know, picking a girl or boy between a certain age . . . usually very young. The older kids were simply taken in to be cheap labour, either at the home or some factory or work mill where they could earn their keep. Siblings like David and Annie often don't end up in the same family.'

'I'm aware of that, but there aren't a lot of options,' Pamela reasoned. 'I take care of them, but when the number gets too high, I can't feed or clothe them. I simply can't handle more than four or five at a time.'

'And to what end?' Sketcher asked. 'Where do they go when they reach their teenage years?' He didn't wait for her to answer. 'They end up working at a menial job for pennies, living in a backroom or attic, growing into an adult with no means to better themselves.'

She sprang to her feet in her own defence. 'It's the best I can do!' she cried – though she kept her voice hushed so it wouldn't carry down the corridor to the living quarters.

Sketcher stood up and stepped over to look down at her. The girl chose to duck her chin and avoid eye contact. He placed his hands to either side of her face and gently coerced her to look up at him.

'What about you, Pamela Hutchings?' he queried gently. 'When do you get a chance to live your own life?'

She immediately lowered her lashes to hide her eyes. In a voice that was a mere whisper, she asked: 'I can read and write enough to get by, but there are few options open to me. I'm living like a mole underground, and there's a reward out for my arrest – what else can I do?'

Sketcher wanted to reach her, to break through her defensive barriers, but he didn't dare come on too strong. If he frightened her, she might ask him to leave.

'I'm an artist,' he said gently. 'I've seen the beauty in a firestorm that levelled a square mile of forest and left only charred remains. I've seen frostbite deform a man's ears and caused the loss of his fingers or toes – yet seen the inner quality of that man, risking his very life for his work, to save the cattle in his care. Whether looking at the heavens, trying to determine how God created such wonders, or the first step of a newborn calf or colt, I see the beauty of life itself. You suffered two great losses in the fire that took your parents – them and yourself. They only lost their lives, while you lost the purpose of life . . . and that is to live it.'

'It's easy to speak of such things, but I couldn't find work after the laundry closed. There are three people for every job and more immigrants coming in all the time. Once McGowan pointed a finger at me I had no choice but to hide.'

Sketcher countered, 'You can't allow that man to determine your future. You deserve a shot at a decent life. I was lucky to end up where I did, but you have a choice – to try and escape your predicament and start anew.'

'I-I was fortunate to escape the fire. My room was at the back of the house. But by the time I got out and tried to get help it was too late.'

Sketcher said carefully, 'But you didn't feel fortunate, did you?'

The young woman took on a look of shame. 'No,' she murmured the word.

'My boss, Reese Valeron, is the nicest guy I ever met,' Sketcher told her. Pam glanced up at him, confused at the complete change of conversation, but he went on. 'He took me under his wing like I was a member of the family and showed me the ropes – everything I needed to know about tending and managing cattle. He had three younger brothers, yet I'm the one he taught to do every job on the ranch. I went from being a stray kid off of the streets to being ramrod over up to thirty men and several thousand head of cattle whenever he's away. I'm actually here in Chicago in his place because he has a wife and wants to stay home with her.'

'What does this have to do with me?'

'Everything,' Sketcher told her. 'Reese married a woman who has memories that are even more painful than yours. The difference is, she got a second chance and took it.'

He went on to explain how Marie had been the victim of an Indian raid, losing her entire family, then ended up a captive and finally a wife to Big Nose, a small-time chief who traded her for a portion of whiskey.

He finished the story with, 'She didn't think herself worthy of a man because of the shame and degradation in her life, but Reese saw beyond her misfortune. The two of them are as happy as any couple in the country.'

'I've tried to find work, but it's a risk every time I leave this place. If I use my name or am seen, I might be arrested. And my kids – I'm the only one who cares if they live or die.'

'I would like to help you, Pamela,' Sketcher said, calling her by her first name. 'My cousins are part of a powerful family. With all of us on your side, we can maybe figure a way to make the wanted poster go away. You deserve a better life . . . the kids, too.'

'Sketcher, I . . .' but the words stuck in her throat.

He rested his hands on her shoulders and looked

directly into her eyes. 'I see you, Pamela, and all of the goodness you cannot hide. I see your compassion, your caring for these homeless children, I see you for the person you are.'

Tears welled in her eyes and she leaned forward. Sketcher slipped his arms around her shoulders as her head came to rest on his chest. Neither said anything for a time, then he began to move in a slow, circular motion, as if they were dancing. It was gratifying to feel the young woman moving in rhythm right along with him.

CHAPTER FIVE

The four Strang boys arrived at Maxine's and were met at the door by Wyatt. For a few tense seconds they simply stared at one another. Finally, Wyatt broke the tension.

'Did your father explain the rules?'

'No beating up the whores,' Aldo said thickly. Then he rubbed the knot on the side of his head. 'And don't expect you to fight fair.'

'You are quite a bit bigger than me, Aldo,' Wyatt replied. 'And I wanted to make a point – I do whatever is necessary to win a fight.'

'We got the message,' the oldest looking of the bunch spoke up. 'Hud and Aldo won't cause any trouble.'

'Like Jack says,' the other young-looking one joined in. 'We behave ourselves or we deal with you.'

'And me,' Tiny added, having come from a place of concealment next to the door. He positioned himself alongside Wyatt.

'Damn!' the third brother – it had to be Carver – declared. 'You're about as wide as an outhouse!'

'You'll think you've fell into one if you test me,' Tiny returned.

'If one of you causes a ruckus,' Wyatt informed them, 'you won't get off with a simple fine. Best understand that before you take another step.'

'We got it, Mr Bouncer,' Hud sneered. 'You done got us skeered to death.'

Jack dug his elbow into his brother's ribs. 'Keep your tongue from wagging,' he scolded him. 'And that goes for you too, Aldo.'

Wyatt moved to the side to allow them to enter. Tiny gave them another once-over and then wandered over to a bar stool in one corner of the room.

As Wyatt kept watch, the four men milled about and then sat down at one of the tables. They spoke to a couple of girls and ordered drinks. Everything seemed cordial and under control.

Wyatt felt a warning stir. The two young hellions were not the kind of men to take a dressing down without retaliating. Hud had the look of a man harbouring a sinister secret. And he had witnessed Aldo's short fuse at work. The older pair seemed peaceful enough, but Wyatt knew there would be trouble down the road. Just how long they would be patient was the only question that needed an answer.

As the evening progressed, only Carver went upstairs with a girl. The other three continued to sit at a table and invited a girl or two to entertain them and bought them drinks. All the while, Wyatt felt ill at ease, wondering what the family had planned.

A bit later, Carver came down to join them. There was some raucous laughter and teasing, but the girl also returned unharmed. It appeared that nothing out of the ordinary was going to happen this night.

'I've got this,' Tiny came to stand next to him. 'Maybe you ought to catch some shut-eye. Doggie just arrived from checking around town. Everything is quiet. Him and me can handle the four Strang boys. They aren't even armed.'

'Their acceptance worries me. If they should start something. . . .'

'You're only a few steps away,' he grunted. 'Don't know how much sleep you'll be getting at nights, not staying out in the back room.'

'Tired as I am tonight, I'll be out like a dead man.'

'I don't think you should use a remark like that around here, Wyatt.'

Wyatt patted him on the shoulder, wandered back to the bouncer's quarters and collapsed onto the bed. He had been getting by on too little sleep ever since he arrived. It was difficult to rest when there were so many possible dangers ahead, but this was the life he'd chosen, the excitement he lived for. Nothing made him feel more alive than to step in and help folks in need. When faced with the odds in Solitary, he wondered if this might be the last job he ever took.

'Where's your head today?' Jared asked Sketcher. 'I go off to talk to a couple of the major buyers and you don't even bid on that last bull?'

'Runner up to the Grand Champion,' Shane spoke in Sketcher's defence. 'It sold for almost two thousand dollars.'

'Pa wanted the best,' Jared reminded them. 'We need to take home at least five or six bulls.'

Sketcher sighed. 'You're right, Jerry. I don't have my

mind on business.'

'This is about the wayward kids and the girl you met,' Jared made the accusation. 'You're still stuck on the idea about clearing her name with the law.'

'I think I've figured a way to do it,' Sketcher said, not denying the conclusion.

Jared grinned. 'Seemed you told me one time that you had no interest in a wife or family. Or is my memory playing tricks on me?'

'The cop is the guilty one,' Sketcher growled, unwilling to admit he had developed a fondness for Pamela. 'That poor girl is caring for a bunch of abandoned kids without a future or hope – not for her or any of them little tykes.'

'OK,' Jared gave in with a sigh. 'What do you have in mind?'

'Another Hereford bull – four years old!' Shane broke into their conversation. 'Shouldn't this wait until. . . .'

Jared glanced at the roan-coloured, stockily built bull that was being led around the auction ring. 'Looks like a good one,' he said to Shane. 'Buy him.'

'Me?' Shane was stunned. 'I'm the horse expert. The only beef I like is when it's served up on a platter with a pile of spuds!'

Jared tapped Sketcher on the shoulder. 'Let's get away from all this noise and discuss your plan.'

'You mean it?' Sketcher was visibly shocked. 'You'll help me do this?'

'I'm not making any promises, but I'll listen to what you have to say.'

The two of them climbed past the benches and the hundred or so buyers, making their way out of the auction house. Once out in the open air, Jared led the way to one of the temporary food and drink places that had been set up to handle the stock show crowd. As there was a major sale going on at the moment, the place had few patrons. They got a table in a corner of the room, ordered a drink, and then got down to business.

Sketcher had confided to Jared about his encounters with the child and the woman who cared for her and three other children. He'd also informed him of her predicament with the law. He outlined what he had in mind and then waited for Jared's opinion.

'So this birthday party for the honcho who runs this part of town is coming up?' Jared pondered the notion. 'That means you don't have much time to get your plan started. How are you going to manage it?'

'Pamela said that Mrs Lannigan has a social circle that meets every Friday night.'

'Meaning tonight,' Jared clarified.

'If I can get my foot in the door, I'll have a good chance of making this work.'

Jared studied him for a moment. 'You've never been in a fight, Sketch,' he said without censure. 'You're talking about risking your very life with this idea. The law in Chicago has a history of being heavily involved with the ruling crime families.'

'Crime families?'

'I remember a few years back, some fellow named McDonald built up something in the news article I read. It was called a gambling and crime consortium.' He grinned, 'Bet you didn't even know I could use a word that big.' He didn't wait for Sketcher to reply, continuing with the story. 'Anyway, they called McDonald's operation 'The Store', and the police chief, William McGarigle, was on the payroll big time. When higher authorities figured out what was going on, the police chief was indicted for graft and fled the country to Canada.'

'Pamela warned me about the same thing. I'm well aware that we can't trust the local law enforcement,' Sketcher told Jared. 'This is the only way I can see to get the job done.'

Jared considered the plan for a few moments and then heaved a sigh. 'It has a chance to work, if everything goes as you hope.'

'I realize there is a risk, but I'm willing to take it.'

'You don't need my approval, Sketch. You have always been one of the family, but you're still your own man. If you need anything from Shane or me, give a holler. Otherwise, the bulls we buy are scheduled for the train ride home in three days.' He wrinkled his brow. 'If you can't rescue Mother and her children from the evil policeman by then. . . .' He shrugged, 'Guess we can cross that stream when we get to it.'

Sketcher chuckled. 'These past couple years, I've dreamed of tagging along with you and Shane, become a part of one of your adventures. Guess my wish is coming true.'

'Not by a long shot,' Jared countered the statement. 'This adventure is all yours. Shane and I have no part in it whatsoever.' Showing a smirk, 'And that's what I'm going to tell Pa if you end up getting yourself killed.'

Because of Sketcher's generosity, Pamela gave the kids a day off from working the streets. She hated to lose the opportunity to hit up the many wealthy stockmen who were on the streets, but the children hadn't had a day of

61

fun since joining her. The four of them played games both inside and out of the burrow. There was food enough to eat, the sunshine was comfortably warm, and she even rounded up enough water so that everyone got to take a bath.

Taking a little time for herself, Pamela cleaned up as best she could and even washed her hair. Donning the one good dress she had – wearing it whenever she had to go buy groceries – she waited with a bated impatience for Sketcher to arrive. He had promised to visit after the stock show and she could not help wondering if he would notice the effort she had put forth to look her very best.

Time passed and darkness forced the children back into the den. After the evening meal, they were all in bed and asleep before Pamela heard the steps coming through the drainpipe. She inwardly frowned as only one candle was burning.

How is he going to see me? She worried.

Sketcher paused at the entrance, adjusting his eyes to the dark interior. Rather than make him stand there idly, uncertain as to what he should do, Pamela picked up the one burning candle and moved over to take his hand. She then led him down the corridor to the same place they had had their first serious and private talk.

'I hoped you would get here a little earlier,' she murmured, carefully placing the candle on the ledge. 'The children wanted to thank you for the food and say good-night.'

'Couldn't be helped,' Sketcher said. 'After the auction, I had to do a drawing or two, and the time got away from me.'

She looked at him expectantly, but didn't hide her

disappointment. 'I understand.'

He displayed regret. 'I would have liked to have eaten with you and the kids. But I have other responsibilities for my employer.'

Pamela said. 'Of course. I told you I understood.'

'I am still looking into your situation, to see if we can find a way to clear your name.'

'It's too dangerous, Sketcher. I'd feel terrible if you got hurt.'

He shook his head. 'I've not had a lot of experience in dealing with criminals and such. The worst critter I deal with is usually a stubborn beef or two. However, I still have an idea that might prove fruitful.'

The girl giggled at his statement. 'I've never heard that phrase – *prove fruitful.*'

'I do a lot of reading, being a bachelor and having my own house. Most of the men bunk together, other than the few married men. I'm about the only one who has a place to himself. Even our two Indians share a cottage. It means I spend a lot of time alone.'

Her features displayed an unfathomable curiosity. 'Why are you so determined to help me?' she asked. 'You will be risking your very life if you get involved.'

'Surely you believe your life is worth a little risk, dear lady.'

'But you don't know me. Until you arrived to sketch the drawing of Annie, you had no idea I even existed.'

'Perhaps it was fate that brought us together,' he said. 'This is the first time I was ever entrusted with coming to one of these stock sales. One of the senior Valerons has always made this trip in the past. And what were the chances I would have parted company with my companions at dusk and happened upon little Annie?'

'You're saying God directed you here?'

He laughed. 'Perhaps He had a hand in it. I often asked if I have a purpose during my prayers, and He is aware of both your plight and my lonely lifestyle. It could be the Man Upstairs took pity on us both.'

Pamela smiled – it was a rare and beautiful smile. 'Were I a suspicious woman, I would think you were using a practised line to win my favour. But,' she added quickly, 'I believe you are sincere.'

'I don't have enough experience around young ladies to have learned the craft of flirting.'

'Me neither,' the girl said. 'Of course, I would be speaking of young men. The only young men I associate with are the ones in the next room.'

Rather than verbally attempt to reassure her, Sketcher moved over and placed his hands on her shoulders. With a slight encouragement, she stepped forward and her head came to rest against his chest.

'I'm frightened,' she murmured. 'Not only for me, but for the children and . . . for you. We are surrounded by dangerous men on both sides. The law throughout much of Chicago is run by crime barons and crooked officials. McGowan would certainly kill you if he thought you were a danger to him.'

'I will be careful not to incur his wrath.'

Pushing back slightly, Pamela lifted her chin and looked at him. 'I want to believe you can help us, Sketcher. But I don't want you hurt. The risk. . . .'

'My dear, Pamela,' he whispered. 'I would risk entering the very halls of purgatory just to hold a girl like you in my arms.'

Rather than debate the plan further, she raised up on her toes, drawn deeper into his embrace. Their kiss was uncertain, both of them lacking experience, but the warmth and emotion smoothed over the singular act of affection, leaving them both content.

Wyatt could not shake the bad feeling he had about the Strang boys. For the second night in a row, the four of them were on good behaviour, not causing a wisp of trouble. Maxine had told him Jack and Carver seldom came to the parlour. Jack was known to be seeing one of another rancher's daughters. She assumed he and Carver were in town to ride herd over Hud and Aldo and see they didn't get into any trouble. The two younger Strangs once again did not take a girl upstairs. It was as if they were avoiding temptation . . . and that didn't fit their personalities. Something was in the wind and it smelled like trouble.

Wyatt left Tiny and Doggie in charge and visited a couple of the other business owners. He suggested they might want to adopt the rules he had put in place. Five men had been killed and another crippled in the past six months over petty or drunken disputes. At the King High, where there was armed security, those men had been forced to kill one man and club down several more when they got out of hand. As most miners didn't carry guns, the killings were mostly done by out-of-control cow hands.

However, even when presented with the violent acts and deaths, the owners were resistant to adopt any rules. They feared retaliation from the ranchers and miners both – all of them opting to keep a wide open town.

It was close to midnight when Wyatt made his last walk

around town. The only action during the evening had been when Tiny had forcibly manhandled a pair of rowdy miners, tossing them both out of Maxine's place. Doggie also disarmed a drunk cowboy who wanted to shoot one of the chandeliers, but it was an unremarkable night.

The routine evening came to an abrupt halt as Wyatt approached the parlour. A man stepped out of the shadows a few steps before he reached Maxine's place.

'Mr Valeron?' the man asked politely.

Wyatt stopped to try and see him more clearly. That's when he realized the gent had a gun pointed at him!

'Can I help you, mister?' Wyatt asked, keeping his right hand near his gun.

'The name's Gino,' he spoke softly, each word uttered like the rustle of leaves in a gentle breeze. 'I'm a range detective for Mr Strang.'

Wyatt tensed, his every nerve on edge. Rather than make a sudden move, he said, 'I'm not in the habit of rustling cattle . . . not from Strang or anyone else.'

'I'm an obliging sort. For the right price, I do whatever is asked of me,' Gino cooed the statement with an icy confidence. 'That's where my work and you collide like a pair of young bulls butting heads.'

Wyatt looked down at his gun. 'Most men shake hands when introduced.'

Having moved into the dull light emitted from Maxine's front window, the man's features were visible. Clad in riding garb, with an expensive flat-crowned hat and a leather jacket, the fellow could have passed as a drummer or gambler. The slender smile on his lips showed more sinister purpose than his amiable tone of voice.

'I told Ed that I'd get rid of you,' he chortled, 'But you're Wyatt Valeron, a man too fast with a gun to give any kind of chance.'

'So why not shoot me in the back?' Wyatt taunted him. 'That's what men like you are good at, isn't it? Why face me and introduce yourself?'

'This has to look like a fair fight,' Gino replied. 'I don't want to be looking over my shoulder for some of your kin the rest of my life. Better if I put a slug. . . .'

Wyatt couldn't see well enough to time the blink of the man's eyes, but he knew he had no other option. He drew his weapon with his incredibly speed—

A blast flashed in his eyes as he felt his own gun buck in his hand! A white-hot pellet of lead tore through his chest and something hit him hard in the head!

Even as a mix of pain and blackness covered his vision and blotted out his thought process, he knew he'd managed to get off a good shot of his own.

The back of his skull bounced off the ground and Wyatt realized he had fallen on his back. A thick fog numbed his brain, preventing any rational thoughts. He'd been gunned down without a chance. His life of taking on the worst of society had finally taken its toll.

The blackness swept over him and swallowed him whole.

Then nothing.

CHAPTER SIX

The banging on the door brought Nash Valeron out of bed. His wife, Trina, also got up and began to don a robe. Any time they were visited in the wee hours of the morning, it meant someone's life was in peril.

Nash opened the door to the waiting area to discover the young town runner who often worked at the express and mail office. His face showed both excitement and concern.

'Telegram just come over the wire!' he practically shouted. 'Wyatt Valeron has been shot!'

Nash snatched the paper from his hand and looked at it. 'Sucking chest wound? He's in Solitude?'

'I had to wake up Mr Rosewood before he could take down the message. Don't hardly ever get a message in the middle of the night. I sleep next to the telegraph in case of emergencies.'

'Go to the stable and wake the liveryman. Tell him I want my horse saddled and ready to ride in ten minutes!'

'You got it, Doc!' the kid replied. Then he raced out into the darkness.

'Did I hear you correctly?' Trina asked, having been

out of sight, wearing a robe over her nightdress. 'Wyatt has a chest wound?'

'A sucking chest wound,' Nash lamented the news. 'If someone there doesn't know enough to seal the wound, the lung will collapse and Wyatt will suffocate.'

'What can I do?'

'Get your shoes on and run over to the telegraph office. I'm sure Rosewood will still be up. Have him send a message to Solitude and tell them to cover the wound to stop the air from escaping. I'm taking a horse and will ride that way as fast as I can. The main road is easy to see at night and it's only about 30 miles. I should be there shortly after sun up.'

'Do be careful, darling,' she said, pausing long enough to kiss him. Then she was hurrying to pull on her shoes.

Nash threw on his riding clothes and grabbed the medical bag he always kept set aside for emergencies. He had everything he would need. His worry was that he didn't know who Wyatt was working for or with, and did any of them know to seal off a sucking chest wound?

The clerk at the hotel hailed Jared over to the counter as he, Shane and Sketcher were on their way out to get breakfast.

'This wire arrived for you a few minutes ago,' the man said. 'I was going to send it up as soon as my help got here.'

Jared opened the telegram marked 'Urgent!' and read it. Shane and Sketcher were both looking over his shoulder and all three felt the impact of the words.

'Wyatt's been shot!' Shane cried out in alarm. 'Holy Hannah! How could that happen?'

'The wire was sent by Brett,' Sketcher observed. 'It says it could be a fatal wound. I'd always thought of Wyatt as bullet-proof.'

'Damn!' Jared groaned his frustration. 'It happened at Solitude – between Cheyenne and Valeron – over a thousand miles away.'

'Take us several days to get there,' Shane agreed. 'When do we start?'

Jared looked at the clock on the wall. 'We need to catch the next train going west. Once headed that way, we can make connections all the way to Cheyenne. From there it's only a half-day's ride to Solitude.'

Sketcher shook his head. 'What about the bulls? We still have to ship the four we've bought and need a couple more.'

'That's on your plate,' Jared told him. 'You take the Wells Fargo voucher and write the check for the ones we've already bought and whatever else you can get. Pa said to come back with at least six prime bulls.'

'OK. I'll take care of it,' Sketcher assured him. 'I know I wouldn't be much help in a fight, so I'm the likely one to stay behind.'

'Plus, you've got the problem to work out concerning that gal you met,' Jared reminded him. 'Try not to get yourself in a bind. There isn't going to be anyone handy to bail you out if you get into trouble.'

Sketcher grinned. 'I'm not a man of violence, Jerry. My plan is one of wit over brawn.'

Jared removed the payment envelope he had been carrying in his vest pocket. He handed it to Sketcher and wished him luck. Then he and Shane hurried up to their room to pack their gear.

Sketcher decided to head for the stockyards. Sometimes a buyer could pick up an animal or two without it going on auction. It saved the seller paying an extra commission, so they both might actually save a few dollars on the purchase. Once he had the bulls lined out and consigned for railroad passage, he could put his plan to help Pamela into action.

He was going to miss the companionship and security of having the two Valerons around, but Jared had outlined the things he needed to know to complete the purchase and transporting of the bulls. If everything went according to schedule, he would finish his business with Pamela and be homeward bound right on schedule.

Nash arrived in Solitude to find Tiny waiting for him. The man took his horse and told him Wyatt was at Maxine's place.

Hurrying to save every second he could, Nash dashed through the door and ran smack into Doggie. The man was quick to recover and caught hold of Nash's shoulders to steady him.

'Easy there, Doctor Valeron,' he said, flashing a wry grin. 'There's no need to rush.'

'The sucking chest wound!' Nash gasped. 'Did you . . .'

'I served during the war,' Doggie told him. 'I knew to protect and seal the chest wound. Remmy is in with Wyatt. We've kept pressure on the wound ever since the shooting.'

'I can't believe it, Dunston,' Nash called him by his actual name. 'Someone actually beat Wyatt to the draw?'

'It was an ambush,' the man replied. 'Reckon there were two of them, 'cause there were three shots right close

71

together – two handguns and a rifle. At least, that's what the livery man said. I was inside the door, it also sounded like three gunshots. Me and the livery man arrived in at Wyatt's side in a matter of seconds. One bullet took your cousin in the chest and a second put a dent in his skull. He ain't come to yet, so we don't know how bad the head wound is.'

'Take me to him.'

Doggie led the way to the back of the building and opened a door to the bouncer's quarters. The girl, Remmy, was sitting with her hand placed on Wyatt's chest.

'I used the heel of my hand at first,' Doggie informed him. 'I had Tiny round up a piece of tin and cut it down to silver-dollar size, then covered the hole. Once it was in place, we wrapped it tight with a bandage.

'We've still been applying steady pressure as a safety precaution, to make sure no air escaped,' Remmy finished the telling of their treatment.

'Good job, Dunston,' then to the lady: 'Ma'am.' Next he looked back at the hired ranch hand. 'But how on earth could you have been in the war? You don't look thirty years old.'

'I lied 'bout my age,' he said. 'I joined at fifteen, along with my two older brothers. Pa was a hard rock miner, so he didn't mind losing three mouths to feed.'

'Praise the Lord for you knowing what to do. You very likely saved Wyatt's life,' Nash affirmed. 'If the lung had collapsed, it would have been the end for him.'

'The head wound isn't too deep,' Remmy advised Nash. 'But it did leave a furrow above his temple and bled quite a bit.'

'It's probably why he lost consciousness,' Nash determined. 'Soon as I finish securing the sucking chest wound, I'll tend to his head.'

'Man has exceptional reaction,' Doggie said in awe. 'Drew and killed the man facing him even as he was getting shot.'

'How do you know that?'

'The livery man I told you about, he saw everything except the second shooter.'

'Well, if I know Jared, he'll be headed this way as fast as he can get here.' He glanced at Doggie. 'Any idea when that will be?'

'He was in Chicago with Shane and Sketcher to buy some Hereford bulls.' Doggie sighed. 'If he'd have been here instead of me and Tiny, no one would have gotten the drop on Wyatt.'

'They were obviously waiting to get Wyatt alone,' Remmy voiced in his defence. 'Even then they were careful to have two guns trained on him. It's a miracle he is still alive.'

Nash checked their patchwork and grunted his approval. 'Looks like a professional patch job, Dunston. Even so, I've got a special patch and liquid sealer I'll use, then sew it into place. I'll also disinfect it as best I can. Was there an exit wound?'

'No,' Doggie said. 'We looked for one but the slug's still in him.'

'Once the seal is in place, I'll have a look. His breathing looks good, so we'll hope the head wound isn't too bad.'

'Sure glad you made such good time,' Doggie said. 'That must have been a long ride in the dark.'

'Yes,' Nash said. 'I was fortunate the trail was clear and the moon was shining. I just pray my trip wasn't wasted.'

'Wyatt's as tough as they come,' Doggie praised the unconscious man. 'With Remmy sitting here fussing over him, he won't dare die on us.'

'Never learned much about moral support in medical school, but I've seen it at work a time or two. Let's hope you're right this time, Dunston.'

Jack confronted Ed after Carver had left the house, along with Hud and Aldo. His father had an odd look about him, as if he had a secret and was afraid to say the wrong word and give himself away.

'Pa,' Jack did not hide his ire. 'What were you thinking? Sending Gino to kill Wyatt Valeron. . . . Are you crazy?'

'It was a fair fight – man to man. They both got off shots and Gino died on the spot. He was supposed to be a better shot.'

'I heard a nasty rumour about a third shooter at the gunfight, Pa.' Jack bored a hole in him with an icy stare. 'Tell me it wasn't you!'

Ed raised and shook his fist. 'That man threatened me, Jack!' he bellowed. 'Stood right in my house and threatened me! No man gets away with that – no man!'

'Hud and Aldo were completely out of hand, Pa,' Jack argued. 'A month ago, those two ganged up on that gambler and killed him. Next thing, the drunken meatheads beat up the sweetest gal working for Maxine, then attacked the bouncer and kicked him to death!' He threw his hands in the air. 'What kind of wild animals have you raised?'

'We already went over this,' Ed dismissed his ire. 'The boys made a couple mistakes. It's regrettable, but just mistakes. As for Valeron, I won't stand for any man talking down to me. Not Wyatt Valeron, not even you!'

Jack took a step back. 'So now you're threatening me? Hud and Aldo started this mess – you and Gino ambush Valeron to make it worse – and you're gonna yell at me?'

Ed simmered. 'No, of course I don't blame you for any of this. But I shouldn't have to defend my actions to you either. Yes, I used the Winchester to make sure the gun-fight went as planned, but . . .' He shook his head. 'Good Lord, Jack! I never knew a man could draw and fire a weapon that fast. I mean, Gino had him cold, gun aimed at his middle, ready to shoot, yet the man pulled iron!' His face displayed disbelief. 'I'd have sworn it was impossible, but Valeron got his shot off at the same instant as Gino. I was so stunned I almost didn't pull the trigger.'

'And you missed.'

'I hit him,' he retorted. 'Damn hard-headed gunman! It only put a dent in his skull.'

Jack rubbed his temples, as if suffering from a headache. 'You know what you've done, Pa. The entire town is going to be swarming with Valeron people.'

'They won't find out it was me,' Ed said confidently. 'It was dark and I had my horse out of sight.'

'Everyone looks out a window or steps outside when they hear shooting, Pa. Someone might have seen you.' Jack's shoulders drooped with his resignation. 'With me and Carver being inside with Aldo and Hud, you're the only one who had motive to kill him, the only one who could have taken the shot. What if the Valerons decide to make a clean sweep and take out all five of us?'

'They would need fifty men,' Ed vowed. 'We've enough guns on this ranch to defeat a small army.'

'Let's hope it doesn't come to that,' Jack said. 'I don't have a lot of confidence when it comes to tangling with that bunch. You heard the story of Brimstone. A hundred outlaw gunmen in that town, yet the Valerons took it without killing anyone except those guilty of kidnapping their kin.'

'Yeah, I heard the story, but I don't believe everything I'm told.'

'Wyatt Valeron killed the Waco Kid in a straight-up gunfight. That much wasn't exaggerated. There was even a news article in the Denver paper about it.' He clicked his tongue. 'It was in a dozen newspapers all over the country.'

Ed skewed his expression. 'After seeing the man draw, that's one thing about the Brimstone story I do believe. I mean, there wasn't even a blur – his draw was faster than that. The gun appeared as if by magic.'

'So what are we gonna do?'

'Nothing to do, son. They can't prove anything, and I've warned Hud and Aldo to stay out of trouble. This will blow over in a week or two and it will be forgotten.'

Jack wanted to believe it, so he let the matter drop. If Wyatt Valeron survived, maybe his killing Gino would be enough to satisfy the rest of the family. If not . . Jack didn't want to think about it.

Sketcher managed to meet and introduce himself to Mrs Lannigan on the night of her social circle. He showed her a couple of his sketches and sweet-talked her into allowing him to draw her. The woman was delighted at his effort and took him to her house to show the piece to her husband. Mike agreed to have Sketcher do a drawing of them both to celebrate his birthday.

Sketcher met up with the happy couple shortly before lunchtime the next day. Mike had the military posture and features of a general. Strong chin, full head of hair, with bold eyes and thick brows, while his wife was the type of subject anyone could make look good. Even having raised four children, she retained a measure of her youthful beauty.

The actual art work took him a full half-hour . . . much longer than usual, but he took care with details and highlighted the couple's best features. His intention was to create a drawing that portrayed the couple in an enhanced, favoured light, and that took a little extra time.

Once finished, he presented his handiwork to them.

'It's wonderful! Marvellous!' Mrs Lannigan applauded his efforts gleefully. 'It's much better than the portrait we had painted of us a few years ago.'

'I work with shades more than colours,' Sketcher explained his craft. 'I've never been very good with paints and oils.'

'It's far superior to anything I expected,' Big Mike agreed with his wife's assessment. 'We must have it fitted with a frame. Its unveiling will be the toast of our banquet tonight. How much do I owe you, young man?'

'I'd settle for five minutes of your time,' Sketcher replied.

Big Mike frowned. 'That's it?'

'That's it, Mr Lannigan. I believe you'll find the conversation quite enlightening.'

'Ilene,' he spoke to his wife. 'How about you take the drawing and round us up a frame. If you have to go to the store, have Louie accompany you.'

77

'That's a wonderful idea, dear,' she said. 'I'm sure we don't have anything in the house worthy enough for your birthday celebration. I'll run down to Lawton's mercantile. He has arts and crafts of all kinds. I'm sure he'll be able to set this in a nice frame for us right away.'

A few moments later, Mrs Lannigan left the house. Big Mike took a seat in a big, comfortable chair and bid Sketcher sit down. Then he leaned forward, businesslike, his flint-like gaze alive with anticipation.

'Now, young man, what about that little talk?'

Wyatt was a little surprised to discover he wasn't dead. It happened that he opened his eyes as Nash and Remmy were discussing the change of dressing for his chest wound. They stopped talking when he blinked and opened his eyes.

'Wyatt!' Remmy cried, throwing her arms around his neck and kissing him about the face and on the lips. When she pulled back enough that his eyes could focus, he saw tears in her eyes. 'I knew you wouldn't die on us,' she murmured in relief.

Wyatt attempted to speak, but his throat was too dry. Nash quickly placed a cup to his lips with a small amount of cool water.

'Hey, cuz,' Wyatt managed, although his words were little more than a whisper. 'How'd you get here?'

'I rode a horse all night just so I could brag to the family how I saved your life.' He grunted. 'Trouble is, Doggie had already controlled the sucking chest wound. I have to give most of the credit to him.'

'I'm not too proud to let a hired hand save my life,' Wyatt said.

'Of course, this young lady also played a part in keeping you alive. Remmy here would make a fair country nurse.'

'Be even better when she can see out of both eyes,' Wyatt teased.

'The swelling has gone down enough that I can see pretty well,' the girl defended her condition. 'I look a whole lot better than you.'

'You always did, little darling,' Wyatt agreed.

'What do you remember?' Nash wanted to know. 'Doggie says he ran outside immediately after the gunshots and found you and another man both lying on the ground. The other man is dead. However, his gun showed only one bullet had been fired, yet you were hit twice.'

Wyatt lifted a hand and touched the bandage that was wrapped around his head. 'Ow!' he said. 'Guess that explains the headache. Man-oh-mama, it feels like someone drove a spike into my skull.'

'Doggie has been checking around, but no one has admitted to seeing anyone else on the street. The livery man witnessed the shooting, but he only saw the two of you. It would seem the second shooter was a ghost.'

'Never believed in ghosts,' Wyatt said. 'When I can get up and around, I'll . . .'

'You're going to stay in bed for a full week. Then you are going to take it very easy — short walks, no excessive exercise — it takes time for a lung to heal. You'll do nothing until the healing of that chest wound is complete.'

'You can't stick around here and baby me along,' Wyatt replied. 'You've got a wife and practice to take care of back in Castle Point.'

'That's why I've instructed Remmy here about your care . . . and precautions. I don't want to have to make the trip back again. You do as I say.' He added, 'You do as Remmy tells you!'

'I'll do the best I can, Nash, but that killer was hired by Ed Strang. Considering his troublesome boys were inside the parlour, I'd wager he's the one who tried to take my head off.'

'Makes no difference, Wyatt,' Nash remained steadfast. 'When Jared gets here, he'll find out who took that shot. You can count on it.'

'Jared's way back in Chicago buying a few prize bulls.'

'Not any more. Locke has been informed of the attack. You will soon have a small army of Valeron people to finish what you started.' He sighed. 'Meaning, I'll likely be back here in a few days to patch up whoever else gets shot.'

Wyatt relaxed at the news. 'Jerry's coming.' With a slender smile playing on his lips, he proclaimed: 'Someone better warn the Strang family . . . hell's fury rides at my cousin's side. And that's the gospel truth!'

CHAPTER SEVEN

The Valeron meeting had the three elder statesmen brothers and many other family members, plus several of those who had known Wyatt for several years. Udal, being Wyatt's father, took charge of the gathering.

'Nash sent a wire this morning,' he began. It caused the twenty or so people outside of the Locke house to grow attentive. 'Nash gives credit to Doggie for saving Wyatt's life. Having been in the war, he'd been around when the treatment for a sucking chest wound was discovered. Nash says Wyatt suffered a wound to the head, too, but thinks my boy will pull through.'

A cheer of relief went up from the group.

'The wire goes on to say that Wyatt killed the man who faced him, but a second shooter is not yet known.'

Locke moved over to stand alongside his youngest brother. 'I sent word to Jared,' he announced. 'He and Shane are Solitary-bound on the train. They should arrive in a couple of days.'

'What are we up against?' Brett Valeron was the one to ask. 'I still have US Marshal authority. What can I do to help?'

81

'You might want to deputize Jared, son,' Locke suggested. 'We don't want any married men risking their lives, but we are going to send a couple of men to help. From what Wyatt said when he asked for Doggie and Tiny, there is a big cattle outfit causing most of the trouble. It could mean dealing with a dozen to fifty men.'

'I'll go!' July volunteered.

'Count me in,' Cliff also voiced his offer. 'The nanny can tend Nessy.'

Several others began to call out, so Locke held up his hands to silence the group. 'Takoda and Chayton . . . Cliff,' he named off his nephew and the two Indian wranglers, 'you three will go.' Then he looked at Reese. 'Who else did you teach to use the gun Nash gave you?'

'Just Landau,' Reese replied. 'I wasn't figuring on ever . . .'

'I'm pretty good with it,' Landau interrupted. 'I'd like to tag along.'

Locke grimaced. 'But you're married to my daughter.'

'Scarlet loves her cousin Wyatt, but her brother, Jared, has always watched over her,' Landau explained. 'If something happened to him because I wasn't there. . . .' He shrugged. 'I've got her blessing to go.'

Locke sought out his eldest daughter. 'Is that right, Scarlet?'

She smiled. 'You have both my and Wendy's blessing, Father. Wyatt and Jared have been there for us when we needed them. We want to help.'

Wendy piped up with, 'Plus Landau is next to Jared when it comes to using a gun. I'm still trying to teach July which end of the gun to point.'

July raised a hand. 'On the positive side, I've learned a

whole lot about numbers and bookkeeping!'

The jest removed some seriousness and allowed everyone to smile.

'You're doing fine where you are,' Locke praised the young man. 'If we need to audit someone to force a confession, we'll send either you or Wendy.'

'I'd send Wendy,' Cliff replied. 'At least she can shoot if it comes to a fight.'

After another short laugh, Locke, Temple and Udal took the volunteers aside and the rest of the family and employees broke up to return to their chores or business.

'You're sure you want to do this, Takoda?' Temple was the Valeron speaking to the Indian wrangler. 'It could be dangerous.'

'Chayton, me, once warriors, then scout for soldiers,' the man answered. 'We hunt many times with Jared – also fight rustlers together. Wyatt, Jared, both blood brothers. We do this for them.'

'All right,' Locke accepted their reason. 'Landau, we know why you volunteered. Get a wagon for supplies. Do you have enough ammo for RJ?'

'About a thousand rounds, Mr Valeron. That ought to be plenty.'

Turning to Cliff. 'You be careful too, Nephew. You are the same as married – you have a child to care for.'

'I want to do my share, Mr Valeron. With Mikki looking after my daughter, I'm sure she will be all right. And I trust Jared. He's got a good head when it comes to any kind of fight.'

'OK, boys,' Locke gave his approval. 'I'm sure Jared will plan with and listen to Wyatt's advice. The two of them have a lot of experience dealing with this kind of thing. We wish you good luck and will pray you all return home safely.'

Sketcher was blindsided by the powerful brute and slammed up against the side of a building hard enough that his breath left his lungs. He was physically spun about and saw who had pushed him, standing face to face with the big cop, McGowan.

'Hello again,' he barely eked out the words.

McGowan threw his forearm up under Sketcher's chin and pinned him snug against the wall. His malevolent face was thrust forward, inches away. The man's breath hit Sketcher in the face and it was laced with the smell of whiskey.

'One of me lads told me you have been gettin' real cozy with Big Mike Lannigan!' he declared. 'Could make a bloke wonder what kind of knavery you are up to, Mr Artist!'

Sketcher swallowed his surprise and mustered up a look of total innocence. 'I did a sketch of him and his wife,' he explained. 'It's what I do to earn some extra money.'

'You claimed to be a big-time cattle buyer!'

Sketcher laughed at the notion. 'Not at all, officer. I merely work on a cattle ranch. I came with the buyers – Jared and Shane Valeron. They are sons of a couple of the Valeron ranch owners. I'm a lowly assistant foreman. I barely earn enough money to live.'

The burly man considered his words and slowly stepped back, allowing him to breathe freely once more. 'The stock sale be about over for beef. I wouldn't like to see you stick around for the hog sale.'

'No, sir,' Sketcher said meekly. 'We made our last purchase today. I will ship out with the half-dozen bulls we bought day after tomorrow.'

'I ain't seen that little scavenger you was drawing the other day,' McGowan said, his eyes full of suspicion. 'You wouldn't be knowin' what happened to the little muffin?'

Sketcher looked around quickly and discreetly lowered his voice. 'To tell you the truth, there's something suspicious about that child's mother – at least, that's what the pixie and a couple other kids call the woman. She seems a most disreputable sort, hiding out in a hole like some kind of animal.'

That perked the man's interest. 'Be you knowing where the gal lives?'

'Yes,' Sketcher answered. 'The little girl led me there. It's rather difficult to get to the burrow where they are hiding.'

McGowan placed his hands on his hips. 'How about you show me the way?'

Thinking quickly, Sketcher again looked around, as if wary of being seen or overheard. 'They have a warning system in place, officer. I would have to get invited back or we would find nothing but an empty cubicle.'

The cop considered the information. 'There be a reward for the lassie who the nits call Mother. I would be willing to split the money with you, if you could arrange a meeting.'

Sketcher pretended to think about it. 'How much of a reward?'

'Your share would be a cool five hundred dollars.'

Flashing a wide smile, Sketcher eagerly bobbed his head up and down. 'For that kind of money, I'm sure I can get us in!' Then putting on a thoughtful frown. 'However, we have to do it carefully – just you and me. If several men showed up, they would scamper away like the rats they eat.'

'When?' the man asked bluntly, confident he could handle one helpless woman.

'I'll search around tomorrow and find one of the waifs. With any luck, I can convince them that I'm willing to pay for another sketching or two.'

'Pray tell, what time do we make this visit?'

'Meet me here at dusk. They always retreat to their hole at dark.'

'Tomorrow. Dusk.' McGowan bore into Sketcher with a hard glare. 'Don't be trying to collect the reward without me. 'Tis a lot of friends I have.'

'Not to worry, officer,' Sketcher replied in a docile voice. 'I'll be here.'

Remmy brought Wyatt his meals during the day. Doggie and Tiny were busy watching the town and trying to find out who the second shooter was. The storekeeper corroborated what the dead man had told Wyatt. He said Strang had been concerned about rustlers lately and hired a range detective named Gino. He confirmed the dead man as being the hired killer. Other than that, the boys had learned nothing.

Wyatt was trying to change position when Remmy appeared in the doorway, carrying a tray with a meal and drink. A tight little grimace darkened her still slightly swollen face.

'What do you think you're doing?' she demanded to know. 'The doctor hasn't been gone for a full day yet and you're trying to undo all of his handiwork.'

'Actually, I was hoping to sit up a little. Maybe I can read something or look out the window. Flat on my back, I'm in a blind spot and can only stare at the ceiling.'

'I'll prop up another pillow for you, but no straining or exerting yourself. You tear that patch your cousin sewed and we'll both be in a world of hurt.'

He smiled. 'You'd make a good nurse, Remmy. You have the charming disposition of an angel ... while remaining a complete tyrant.'

She set the tray on the nightstand and moved to the head of the bed. By lifting Wyatt by his shoulders, the two of them managed to get a second pillow wedged in behind him. As he reclined, he was able to see out the window – though there was nothing but the side of a hill visible.

He looked at Remmy and saw she had her hand placed against her side. 'Oh, damn!' he exclaimed. 'I forgot about your cracked ribs. That had to have hurt something fierce.'

She smiled to dismiss his concern. 'We make a good pair, both of us crippled up until we can hardly get around.'

He waited until she had placed the tray on his lap before he spoke. 'You're a good woman, Remmy ... or whatever your real name is.'

She sat on the chair next to the bed, ready to hand him the drink when he wanted, patiently allowing him to eat at his own pace. At his remark, she had grown pensive. The pause was long enough Wyatt about forgot the subject until the girl finally broke the silence.

'My maiden name was Remington,' she said quietly.

'Valerie Remington.'

He suspended the bite inches from his mouth and repeated the incredulous statement. 'Your *maiden* name?'

'I am married.' She considered the statement and clarified, 'I *was* married. It wasn't a good marriage, nor was it the worst marriage,' she related. 'But the man my father chose for me was very rigid in his manner and expected certain things from a wife. One of those things was that she bear him a house full of children.'

The young woman remained somber, so Wyatt did not encourage her to continue. He realized this was very difficult for her. After a short hesitation she began again.

'I did try to please him until I conceived with our first child. That's when everything went wrong. The local doctor told me the baby was growing outside the womb. Not only wouldn't it survive, but neither would I.' Her voice cracked with emotion. 'I kept hoping a miracle would happen, but then . . .' She swallowed another sob at the memory. 'Once there was no longer a heartbeat for the child, the doctor did what he had to in order to save my life.'

'I'm so sorry, Remmy,' Wyatt tried to comfort her with his empathy. 'But it was nature's mistake – it wasn't your fault.'

The muscles tightened along her jaw as she grit her teeth. 'It was my fault . . . according to my husband. When the doctor told him I could never have children, he practically attacked him. He ranted about fatherhood and continuing his legacy, about the help he would need running our farm. He refused to give up his dream of a big family because of my failure as a mother.'

'What a callous, unfeeling swine!' Wyatt declared.

'There are orphaned or discarded kids in every city or town. He could have adopted a dozen children.'

Remmy sighed. 'They would not have been good enough for him. He wanted his bloodline to continue.'

'What did he do about a divorce?' Wyatt wanted to know. 'You can't just throw out your wedding vows and remove your name from the courthouse marriage records.'

'That's precisely what he did,' Remmy informed him. 'My husband had me listed as dead and declared himself a widower. He stuck me on the stage with one suitcase and a ticket to Cheyenne. Maxine happened to be in town shopping and saw me walking the streets crying. She took me in and . . . well, after a time, I had to earn my keep doing more than just cleaning up at nights.'

'You never struck me as a woman who would choose this sort of life,' Wyatt told her. 'I mean, you don't drink hard liquor and you're not loud or vulgar. It's why I was drawn to you.' He laughed at the next words, but said them with sincerity. 'You are something rare in your field, Remmy – a nice girl.'

She laughed too, though tears still glistened in her eyes. 'Yes, every man comes to a parlour like Maxine's to find himself a *nice* girl!'

Wyatt had finished eating. He took a drink from the cup she had brought him and then leaned against the pillows. 'Tell you one thing, Remmy,' he said. 'This is the first time a bullet ever put me flat on my back. I've had a nick or two, but this time . . . it might be the Lord warning me to change my ways.'

That put a smile on her lips. 'I like the way you think the Lord takes care of you. With some men, assuming they were somehow special in the Lord's eyes would be a sacrilege, but I believe it when you say such a thing.'

'The Lord loves us all, Remmy. But that doesn't mean He likes or approves of some of the things we do. Remember, He is our Father in Heaven. A good father forgives his child's mistakes or sins.'

'So He will forgive me for being a harlot?'

'Jesus forgave Mary Magdalene.'

Remmy arched an eyebrow. 'Yes, but He also told her to sin no more,' she grunted. 'How am I supposed to go and sin no more while I'm doing what I am to keep from starving on the streets?'

Wyatt gazed at her, enjoying every minute detail about her face, her expression, the rings of gold within her cloudy blue eyes. This was a woman he cared about, a woman he had risked his life to protect. If he were ever to take a wife. . . .

'What?' Remmy asked, frowning at the strange look on his face. 'What is it, Wyatt?'

'Uh, nothing,' he dismissed the issue. 'I had a passing thought, but it's too silly to even say aloud.'

Remmy leaned over and kissed him on the cheek. The act obviously caused her some discomfort. In spite of her lip having returned to normal size, there was still a crack that hadn't healed completely.

'Get some rest,' she coaxed gently. 'I'll be back in a while and we can play some cards or something. I don't want you getting bored and trying to get out of bed.'

'Yes, nurse,' he said patiently. 'I'll do just as you say, nurse.'

She rewarded him with another of her pleasing smiles and left the room.

Wyatt stared at the closed door for a long time. Remmy stirred emotions in him he had never before experienced. The more he thought about it, the more he didn't want her sharing favours with another man . . . not now . . . not ever!

Sketcher spent the morning finishing up at the auction. After writing a pay voucher for the six bulls they had purchased over the duration of the sale, he arranged to have them sent to the loading docks. The critters would have tags and numbers, corresponding to the rail car into which they would be loaded. He visited the train station and checked the travelling arrangements so both he and the cattle would be on the same train. It was afternoon before he wrapped everything up, so he prepared for his last night in Chicago.

He sent off a telegraph message to the Valeron ranch, so Locke could arrange for final transport of the cattle once they reached Wyoming. With his business concluded, he then bought some groceries and went to visit Pamela and the children.

A warmer greeting a man never had, four children crowding around him, each wanting to give him a hug. As for Pamela, she remained more subdued, knowing this would be his last day in town.

The woman prepared a nice meal and the kids all laughed and enjoyed eating their fill. Their gaunt little bodies had responded nicely to a few meals, consuming all they wanted. Plus, being able to play for a few hours, rather than spend all of their time on the streets selling matches, flowers or apples, it had added dramatically to their overall health and well-being.

Once alone with Pamela, Sketcher took her by the hand. They walked down the corridor to her private place and sat together on the wooden crate she used as a chair.

'This is it, isn't it?' Pamela said after an awkward silence. 'You will be leaving tomorrow.'

'Everything is scheduled,' he replied. 'The bulls are in the holding pen and have a designated car. Nothing left to do but get them home.'

She regarded him with a timid, yet dimpled simper. 'You've been like a foster father to the children these past few days. I've never seen them so happy.'

'They are wonderful kids.'

'Is there any chance you will return next year?'

'It depends on how everything works out,' he evaded.

'I . . . I never let a man kiss me before,' she said. 'However, I don't want you thinking you owe me anything. You've been a godsend for me and the children, but there is no obligation, no bond between us other than friendship.'

He smiled at her. 'You are a treasure, Pamela. You have dedicated your life to tending to some of these street urchins and very probably saved their lives.' He sobered to add: 'But this is not a suitable life for you, nor for them.'

'I know, Sketcher. Yet the alternatives for abandoned children are not good. So many of them are forced to live on the streets, some stay with their mothers in the county poorhouse, or wind up in jail or the Chicago Reform School, because there is not enough room in institutions for all of the homeless children.' She sighed, 'I guess I don't have to tell you this. You suffered through the ordeal of the orphan and displaced children's train, being sent down the tracks in the hopes of finding a home.'

'I was one of the lucky ones,' he admitted. 'But you can't forfeit your own life trying to shelter a few street kids. You should have a chance at happiness and perhaps a family of your own.'

'There is a reward out for my capture . . . remember?'

Sketcher placed his hand over her own. 'That is something you need to face. You can't hide in this hole forever.'

'And how do I go about that?' she wanted to know. 'Do I turn myself over to the law and face a judge and jury? Do you really think they would believe my story over that of a policeman? And what would happen to my children? They would be stuck on one of those trains!'

'I've got to go down to the loading docks and check on those bulls,' Sketcher said, not responding to her questions. 'I should be back about dark.'

She looked into his eyes as if trying to read something he was hiding. 'All right,' she said, obviously not pleased at how this sit-down had turned out. She let him walk away without another word, probably wondering if he would come back or not.

Because of what lay ahead, Sketcher dared not linger a moment longer. After this night, Pamela might be relieved her hiding days were over, or she might hate him for being a traitor. Regardless, he had to do what he thought was best for her . . . and for the children.

CHAPTER EIGHT

Landau pulled the buckboard over to the alleyway next to Maxine's place. A large canvas was tied down over the bed, covering the supplies, miscellaneous gear and bedding they had brought along. Cliff and the two Indians remained atop their horses as Doggie and Tiny came rushing outside to greet them.

'I thought they were sending us some help,' Tiny jeered. 'All I see is a couple over the hill Injun scouts, an old married man, and a carousing young buck who ain't worth a pinch of salt. What was Locke thinking?'

'He was thinking anything was an improvement over you two,' Cliff retorted. 'You came here to help Wyatt – and you helped get him shot!'

Both men started to alibi at once, but Landau climbed down and raised a hand to silence their excuses.

'How's he doing?' he asked. 'Nash wired that Wyatt had a close call with death.'

'Wait 'til you see his nurse,' Tiny replied. 'I don't know a man on this earth who wouldn't stick around with her watching over him.'

94

'Yeah,' Doggie chipped in. 'That Remmy is 'bout as sweet and purty as any gal you ever set your blinkers on.'

'Nash did mention how you saved Wyatt's life,' Landau directed the words to Doggie. 'That helps even the score for allowing him to get shot in the first place.'

'Trick I learned during the war,' the man informed them.

'And you call me an old married man! You must have ten years on me.'

Doggie grinned. 'I lied about my age when I joined up – told 'um I was sixteen, when I was really only twelve.'

Tiny grunted. 'Last time he told the story he was fourteen. Pretty soon, he'll be saying he was still wearing short pants and barely walking good.'

'The number of years a person lives doesn't necessarily determine his age,' Doggie turned philosophical. 'Look at Cliff here . . . he tips the age scale at somewhere in his early twenties, yet still acts like he is fourteen.'

Most of them laughed. Cliff showed a good-natured grin. 'Never changes – it's always "pick on Cliff" because he's the youngest.'

'Good reason to keep you around,' Landau joked.

'So, is there any word from Jared and Shane?' Cliff turned serious.

'On their way, so the last telegraph message said,' Tiny answered the query. 'Should be here sometime tomorrow or the next day.'

'Where do we bunk?' Landau asked. 'I need to put RJ in a safe place.'

Tiny frowned. 'You brought Reese's toy along?'

'Someone said we might have a war on our hands,' Landau responded. 'Have to make up for the poor quality

95

of our fighting force, and RJ is a dandy equalizer.' Then he looked at the biggest man from the Valeron spread. 'Uh, no offence, Tiny.'

'None taken,' he replied. 'I'm not much of a hand in a gunfight.'

Landau wiped his brow and looked around. 'Where are we staying?'

'At the old trading post, up at the edge of town,' Tiny informed him, pointing down the street. 'There's plenty of room, but we have to bed down on the floor. Just find a comfortable spot and toss your gear. The grub house across the street is passable.'

'Meaning we'd *pass* it up if there was anyplace else in town to eat,' Doggie quipped.

'Long as we've got food and shelter, we'll get by,' Landau said. 'Any plan in place yet?'

'Yeah,' Tiny replied. 'We keep an eye on things and wait for Jared.'

Landau chuckled, 'Seems the smart thing to do.'

'Next to Wyatt,' Cliff said, 'he's the one I'd follow when taking on an unfriendly town or a ranch full of gunmen.'

'Think we might have both of those right here,' Tiny threw the notion into the banter. 'Doggie can keep watch here and I'll help you guys get settled.'

'Lead the way,' Landau said. 'Takoda has been complaining about not having anything to drink for the last twenty miles.'

'They might not serve Indians at the saloon,' Tiny warned.

'I'll buy them each a bottle of beer, soon as we stow our gear,' Cliff volunteered.

'Clifford is new best friend!' Takoda proclaimed.

'Only till the bottle is empty,' Landau joked. 'Only till the bottle is empty.'

At McGowan's approach, Sketcher took a deep breath and let it out slowly. He'd listened to the many tales of Brett, Jared and Wyatt, of their daring deeds and brushes with death. For the most part, he had enjoyed their adventures, often visualizing the experience and wondering how the danger and excitement must have felt. Well, this was real, and he was sweating like a bronc buster in midsummer, his heart hammering like a dozen men driving railroad spikes, and he could hardly suck a breath of air into his lungs. He feared his knees would buckle under him and reverently prayed his voice and courage didn't fail him.

'I come alone,' was McGowan's greeting. 'But I've a good many mates, so you don't want to try anything stupid.'

'I'm only here on behalf of those wayward children,' Sketcher assured him. 'The sooner this is over, the better.'

'Be a shade richer too – five hundred dollars when the bounty is paid. How many drawings would that be taking you?'

Sketcher managed a tight grin. 'About five hundred.'

'Now where be this hidey-hole you was tellin' me about?'

Sketcher took the lead and wound through the back alleyway and around piles of discarded trash and other debris. Reaching the large drainage pipe, he paused.

'You have to duck low, but it's only a few steps. We must move quietly or they will hear us coming.'

'Any place for them to run?'

97

'Not unless they get past us. The room is full of pipes and quite large, but this is the only way in or out.'

'The street woman is the only one I'll be wanting. You can do with the little beggars as you see fit.'

'The kids shouldn't be a problem,' Sketcher said. 'The oldest child is only about eight years old.'

'Lead the way, artist,' McGowan ordered.

Sketcher proceeded to the cardboard-covered entrance. 'It looks solid,' he whispered to McGowan, 'but the barrier is there to keep out the cold. Are you ready?'

'Let's go,' he ordered. 'This bending down is breaking my back!'

Sketcher mustered his spirit and pushed aside the barricade. As he entered, Pamela's face lit up with a smile of greeting—

McGowan pushed past Sketcher and the children all began to scream. They ran to the sheltering arms of Pamela and her expression morphed into shock. Rather than look at the policeman, she stared in horror at Sketcher.

'How could you?' she wailed. 'We trusted you!'

Sketcher held up both hands to try and calm her. 'It's for the best,' he said quickly. 'You can't live in this hole like some kind of animal. You have to face this charge and put it behind you.'

'I'll end up in prison!' she cried. 'I told you – I didn't do anything. That man you're with – Officer McGowan – he's the one who killed Rufe Lannigan! He was afraid I'd seen him do it, so he blamed me!'

'Now, lassie,' McGowan said gruffly. 'You do and say what I tell you and you'll be a free woman in a few months.'

'I committed no crime!'

He held up his hands to quiet her and the children. 'You tell the judge that Rufe grabbed you on the street and began to paw at you. You were defending your honour. It makes his death self-defence.'

'You gave me the knife you used to kill him!' she snapped at the cop. 'I found blood on it when I got home!'

' 'Tis your word against mine, little scavenger,' McGowan guffawed. 'No judge would be believing you over me.'

'Perhaps the young lady could say she witnessed the fight?' Sketcher posited. 'If you had no choice, officer, wouldn't the law find you innocent?'

'Big Mike don't care about details, artist,' he snorted the words scornfully. 'He's all about making someone pay for his loss. The lassie can say whatever she pleases, so long as she don't point her finger at me.'

'But the truth . . .'

'Listen, artist!' McGowan bellowed. 'You just take your share of the reward money, catch your train home and keep your mouth shut!' Then glaring at Pamela. 'And you, Scavenger . . . you will do like I say, or else these four gutter-rats are going to end up in the worst pest hole for kids the city has to offer. They'll be lucky to see another summer!'

Pamela, her eyes filled with tears and her face twisted in anger and dread, burned a searing hole in Sketcher. 'See what you've done?' she sobbed. 'You've doomed us all!'

'I'm sorry, ma'am.' Sketcher attempted a display of sincerity. 'I was thinking of your welfare, and it is the only way to save you and the children from this terrible existence.'

'Come with me, scavenger,' McGowan commanded Pamela. 'You tell the story the way I told you – Rufus laid hands on you and you fought back. At most, you might get a coupla years.'

'But you're the one who killed him, not me!'

'Tut, tut, little beggar. I only done what I had to do.' McGowan pointed his finger at her. 'Now, be a good lassie. Don't make me drag you out of here in front of the kiddies.'

'Them be the very words I was going to use for you, Gruff McGowan,' a cool voice said from behind Sketcher and the policeman.

All eyes turned to see two of Big Mike's men – previously introduced to Sketcher as Louie and Duffy – at the entrance way.

The cop's eyes grew as big as silver dollars. He stared at Sketcher and fury distorted his features. 'Artist!' he roared. 'You dirty, underhand—' He made a lunge for Sketcher, but was too slow.

Louie darted between McGowan and Sketcher, as Duffy produced a gun.

Sketcher jumped back out of the way so the two men could take charge of the guilty policeman.

'I never liked you much, you big Irish bully,' Louie sneered into the man's face. 'It's going to be a real pleasure watching you explain to Big Mike why you killed his cousin.'

'Wait a minute, boys!' McGowan's bravado vanished. 'It wasn't a killing on purpose! Rufus attacked me! I was defending myself!'

'I'm sure Big Mike will want to hear all about it,' Duffy said, sticking the gun against the man's ribs. 'Let's go see if he believes you.'

With those words, he pushed McGowan back out the entrance way. Louie remained in the den for a moment and looked around.

'Sorry you've had to live like this, Miss,' he spoke to Pamela, showing a trace of compassion. 'Big Mike promised to clear your name first thing in the morning.' Then he pulled an envelope from his pocket and handed it to Sketcher. 'He thanks you again, too.' With a grin, 'Also, I have to tell you, that was one dandy drawing of the boss and his wife. You've got real talent.'

'Thank you,' Sketcher replied. 'I'm glad everything turned out the way it did.'

Louie grunted. 'Yeah, everybody's happy but Gruff McGowan. I can't say I'm surprised. He always did think too much of himself.'

'I appreciate you boys stepping in before he had a chance to remove my head from my shoulders,' Sketcher said.

Louie raised a hand in a short wave and followed after Duffy and McGowan. Behind him there remained a stunned silence, with Pamela and the kids still dumb-founded about what had just happened.

Sketcher waited until the six of them were alone before he cleared his throat to explain.

'I . . . I didn't dare tell you of my plan,' he began. 'It had to look like you believed I had betrayed you. If Officer McGowan had realized this was a trap, a way to coerce a confession, it. . . .'

But Pamela broke free of the children and charged the

few steps between them. She ploughed into him as she threw her arms around his neck. Sketcher was knocked back a step but regained his balance, just in time to be kissed full on the mouth. Even as he enjoyed the delightful contact, the kids all gathered around giggling and chattering with excitement.

'You see?' Monte was telling the others. 'Didn't I tell you? Mr Sketcher said he would help us and he did!'

'You risked your life!' Pamela murmured next to his ear. 'McGowan has a lot of friends. It was a very dangerous plan. Once word gets around . . .'

'I'll be long gone,' he dismissed her warning. 'The train leaves tomorrow at noon. By the time McGowan's pals learn of his plight, I'll be out of the city and on my way home.'

The young woman unfurled her embrace and stepped back. Her eyes still glistened with emotion, while a mixture of affection and concern was ingrained in her features.

'Yes,' she said softly, the regret evident in her voice. 'I suppose you are right.'

'But what about these friends of McGowan's? Is there a chance they might want to get even with you and the children?'

'I don't know,' she answered. 'Me, possibly, but I shouldn't think the children are in any danger from them.'

Sketcher reached out and pulled Pamela back into his arms. 'Well, I intend to make certain you are all right . . . you and the kids, too.'

She studied him with an intense scrutiny. 'What are you talking about?'

'I've got the reward money for Rufus Lannigan's killer here – one thousand dollars!' He asserted. 'You can take the kids and set yourself up in a place where the kids can go to school and you can take care of them. You can move away from this city, go someplace else and get a fresh start.'

When he didn't proceed, she wrinkled her brow in puzzlement. 'I-I don't know what . . .' She fumbled for words. 'A thousand dollars?'

'That's about a year's salary for me,' Sketcher said. 'It will take care of you and the kids for a good long time.'

'But . . .' she struggled with the decision. 'I mean, what about the debt I owe you?'

'You don't owe me a thing, Pamela. I've been more than happy to help,' he chuckled. 'It's one tale I can tell around the camp-fire to equal that of some of the Valerons.'

'Then you're returning home as scheduled?'

'The Valerons entrusted me with their new Hereford bulls. It's my job to see they get safely to the ranch.'

Pamela was in a total daze, unable to think or put together another sentence. As she struggled to comprehend having such a great deal of money, little Annie walked over and tugged on Sketcher's pant leg.

'You gonna leave us?' she asked, displaying a worried look.

Sketcher gazed at Pamela. 'I'm not responsible for you, your brother and the other kids, Annie. The decision about where you go or what happens next is up to Mother.'

Annie stared up at Pamela with her large eyes. 'Mother, can we go with Daddy?'

103

CHAPTER NINE

Jared and Shane arrived to find Cliff and Landau sitting on the front porch of the old trading post. They moved out to meet them as they dismounted from their jaded mounts.

'You made good time,' Cliff said. 'We only got the telegraph message from Brett a couple hours ago.'

'I wanted some kind of authority,' Jared said. 'Brett deputized me so I could arrest the man responsible for the attempted murder of Wyatt.'

Landau grunted. 'The Jared I know never bothered to arrest the guilty – he hung 'um.'

Jared grinned. 'Yeah, well I'm not expecting anyone to give up without a fight.'

'That's why we brought RJ,' Landau retorted. 'Reese gave me a little training and I think it can help us – either to avoid an all-out war, or to win one.'

Jared stated: 'First thing, I'm going to speak to Wyatt. Shane can put up our horses. It'll be dark soon, so we'll catch up with what all you've learned over a meal.' He pointed up the street. 'That the only eating place?'

'They put out decent food. Pricey, but edible,' Cliff

made the reply.

Jared left them and walked down to Maxine's parlour. He had been there a couple times with Wyatt, but only to socialize. He often tipped the girls generously, but paying for favours was something he didn't do. It was a personal thing; he didn't judge anyone else by his own standards.

Maxine recognized him and hurried over to give him a hug – she always greeted him and Wyatt with a warm squeeze and a bright smile. She stepped back and surveyed him from head to foot.

'You look like you've been on an all-night drunk for about three days, Jared.'

'Feels like it, too,' he told her. 'Trains might be faster than horses, but I can throw a blanket on the ground and be a whole lot more comfortable than trying to sleep on one of those wooden-slab benches. I'd rather take a beating than do that again.'

'Wyatt is doing just fine. Nash patched the wound and managed to remove the bullet – it had lodged near the surface in his back – and Remmy has been a dutiful full-time nurse.' She winked. 'I wouldn't be surprised if she leaves this line of work. The two of them have become very close.'

'He always called Remmy his best girl,' Jared confided to her. 'Whenever he got the urge for companionship, this was his first choice.'

'I won't keep you, dear,' she said. 'Wyatt is in the bouncer's room at the back. He'd only just taken on job of bouncer a couple days before he got shot.'

'Didn't do much of a job, did he?' Jared complained. 'I'll be sure and tell him you're going to hire someone better qualified once he heals.'

She laughed. 'Yes, do that.'

Jared passed by a couple of parlour girls. It was not yet dark, so it was quiet. One of them gave him a smile of greeting, but it was strictly professional. He didn't recognize either of them from his last visit.

Remmy about ran into him as he reached the doorway, leaving Wyatt's room with a tray and some empty dishes.

'Jared!' she exclaimed happily. 'I'm so glad to see you!'

'Nice to see you too, Remmy.'

'No,' she countered, looking deadly serious. 'I mean it. I've been worried to death one of Strang's men would try to finish what they started. I wouldn't put it past them to shoot him through the window or sneak in at night and cut his throat.'

'They won't be getting a second chance, not with me and some of the others here,' Jared vowed. 'Before I'm through, the Strang family will be as tame as a herd of lambs.' He gave a grim chortle. 'Or they'll be buried six feet underground.'

An appreciative simper came to her lips. 'Same ole Jared that Wyatt has talked about ever since we met. He always said you'd have given Judge Parker – known as the hanging judge – a run for his money. Except you prefer to do the hanging yourself.'

'I never once hanged a man who wouldn't have suffered the same fate after a trial. Guilty is guilty. No need taking a chance on an escape or crooked judge or jury, where the condemned man might go on to harm or kill another innocent victim.'

'Yes, I understand your logic . . . barbaric as some may think it is.'

He took a closer look at the woman. 'I see what started

all of this. It's lucky whoever beat you didn't damage the eye socket. I've seen skulls that cracked or broken facial bones only the best surgeons can mend. Any man who harms a woman or child . . .' He didn't have to finish, the dark expression on his face stated his position.

Remmy smiled again. 'It really is good to see you, Jared. Maybe Wyatt will be able to sleep more peacefully now.'

Jared went past her and entered Wyatt's room. He'd seen his cousin after a fight or injury before, but he'd never seen him so completely vulnerable. Wyatt had always been so careful, so gifted with a gun. Jared had thought of him as being immortal. Now, having barely escaped death. . . .

'Jerry!' Wyatt greeted, lifting a hand.

Hurrying over to his bedside, Jared took the hand in a firm grip. 'Dad-gum, Wyatt,' he jeered. 'Is this the only way you could figure to spend time with Remmy? Make her your personal nurse!'

'Worked pretty good,' Wyatt said back, '. . . other than for the sucking chest wound. I'm glad they waited to ambush me until Tiny and Doggie were here. Dog served in the war and knew to seal the wound and apply pressure.' He laughed without humour. 'Bet it was something to see – Dog, Tiny and Remmy, all taking turns holding a patch over my wound.'

'What about that bandage on your head, just above your ear?' Jared gestured at the bandage. 'Any of your brains fall out?'

'That's a souvenir from a second shooter I didn't see. He fired about the same time as the guy who faced me.'

Jared frowned. 'I can't believe the guy outgunned you.'

'He didn't,' Wyatt replied. 'He started out with his gun pointed at me. I had to draw and shoot before he could pull the trigger,' he sighed. 'Guess I'm not that fast. He got off a shot of his own. But it was the second gun – probably a rifle from a short way off – that I didn't see. He put my lights out when that bullet about removed my ear.'

'No one saw who it was?'

'Dog and Tiny haven't had any luck finding a witness. Landau and Cliff have also checked around some. Either the man had a partner or one of the Strang family took a hand. If I was to guess, I'd put money on Ed, the father of the pack of wolves. He struck me as a man who didn't like to lose an argument, and I collected five hundred dollars from him for damages done by two of his sons.'

'You can rest easy from here on, cuz,' Jared promised. 'Won't be no rest for whoever was behind that rifle. He doesn't know it yet, but he's a walking corpse.'

'Now, Jer, I see you're wearing a badge. A deputy US Marshal is supposed to represent law and order. Brett won't be happy if you cross the line.'

'I took the job for the authority it carries,' Jared grinned back. 'Guess my brother will have to cover for anything I do that crosses one of those lines.'

'Maybe you should give the badge to Shane, he'll stick to the rules.'

'Shane will do as I tell him, the same as always, Wyatt.' Jared reached out and patted his cousin on the shoulder. 'You just worry about getting better . . . and wallowing in the affection you're getting from Remmy. That's your only job until this is over.'

'When you put it that way, give 'um hell, Jerry!'

*

108

Carver came to the supper table late. Ed looked up to see he had an unhappy expression on his face.

'You're late,' Ed muttered. 'The cook went home soon as the table was set. He seems a mite skittish lately.'

'He has probably been listening to the riders who've been eating or drinking in town,' Carver replied. 'Solitary is crawling with gunmen – a couple of them with the last name of Valeron.'

Ed took a bite and chewed, not bothering to comment.

'Anyone get a count yet?' Jack asked his brother.

'Two Valerons, plus the two men who had been in town to help Wyatt, and at least four more – two of which are Indians.'

Aldo laughed his contempt. 'Hot damn! Them boys must be scraping the last jam from the jar. Indians don't know squat about gunfighting!'

'Yeah,' Hud joined in. 'Maybe they hired them to come around here and smoke a pipe to make peace.'

Carver looked at Jack and cocked his head in the direction of their younger brothers. 'These two lamebrains ain't got a clue as to what kind of fight might be ahead. We're not talking a couple of farmers. These are the Valerons! According to what we've heard about them, they've tamed a bandit town, busted up a rustling operation and shut down the Paradise mining operation the other side of Denver. Each of those gangs of outlaws had a pile of money and guns, and every single one of them wound up in prison or dead.'

'Carver's right,' Jack declared. 'You two started this, but it's going to take us all to put an end to it.'

'You're sounding all kinds of scared,' Aldo taunted him.

'Jack and Carver are maybe gonna turn us in and hope there's a reward!' Hud threw in a jeer of his own.

Ed slammed his fist down on the table with enough force that everyone grew instantly silent. There was no humour in his expression, only a dark light burning in his eyes.

'This here ain't no teasing game, boys,' he stated grimly without raising his voice. 'We need to set up a defence and be ready. It's only a matter of time before them Valerons show up and try to arrest you two . . . and me as well.'

'You?' Carver asked, incredulous. 'Why should they come after you?'

'Because I shot Wyatt Valeron at the same time as Gino. If they don't already know it was me, they are bound to be thinking it. We've got to set out a couple wagon loads of grain for cover. We need to reinforce the shed and barn with extra lumber so the walls will stop bullets.'

'You really serious about this?' Aldo asked, displaying total disbelief.

'Damn right!' Ed avowed. He looked at Jack. 'Put a couple of men scouting the hills, to warn us if they approach, and I want no less than ten men here at the ranch at all times.'

'Holy hell, Pa!' Hud exclaimed. 'With that many men tied up, there ain't gonna be enough left to watch over the herd!'

'If they hit us, I intend to be ready.'

'We don't have a lot of gun-toting cowhands,' Carver warned. He looked at Jack. 'How many can you think of?'

Jack scratched his head in thought. 'There's Wade, Cy, Darth . . . Sanders, and maybe Sonny – those are about the only men I can think of who are much good with a gun.'

'How about Gus and his three cousins?' Carver wondered aloud.

'No,' Jack replied. 'Gus is a good foreman and dedicated cow man, but he don't know squat about fighting a battle. Three of the others I mentioned did some injun fighting, but none of them signed on as gun-hands.'

Ed growled, 'This is about protecting ourselves from outsiders, a handful of men who think they can impose laws and rules that we have to obey.'

'You mean like not knocking around a parlour girl?' Jack shot back cynically. 'Or ganging up on a bouncer or gambler to kill them? How about shooting a man from ambush? Is that the kind of rules you're against, Pa?'

'The boys were drunk,' Ed battled back. 'All right! They got a little carried away, but we're only talking about a whore, a couple of unknowns and some wandering gunman. We're supposed to change the rules we've had for ten years for those three?'

Jack laughed, but it was not mirth, it was due to the argument. 'Call me pious if you want, but I always thought that not hurting or killing people was the kind of a rule all men tried to live by . . . without needing the Valerons to step in.'

'Hud and Aldo have promised to behave!' Ed said emphatically. 'That ought to be the end of it!'

'Shooting a man from ambush isn't the right way to end an argument, Pa. The Valerons are going to find out it was you; they are going to want their pound of flesh.'

Ed scowled at him. 'If you'd listen instead of yak all the time, you'd have heard me when I said it's why I want a dozen men, ready to fight, ready to defend the ranch against an attack by the Valerons.'

Jack lifted his hands in surrender. 'Whatever you say, Pa. We'll do it your way. I'll round up the men and have them set up barricades and whatever else you think we need. If the Valerons come after you three, I reckon we will deal with them.'

There were an inordinate number of police at the railroad station. Sketcher's nerves caused a roil within his gut and his heart pounded so hard he had to forcibly ignore the thunder claps resounding in his head. A beefy cop stood at the station window glaring about as if ready to dismantle the first person to look crosswise at him.

Sketcher approached the window, relieved to see the agent was the same man he had spoken to about the travelling arrangements for the bulls. His name was Davis and he had put on extra security due to the value of the Hereford cattle. Sketcher didn't miss the cop's circumspect glance as he walked up to the opening.

'Is everything in order, Davis?' Sketcher asked, the nervousness imbuing his words. 'I see a number of police. It doesn't concern my shipment does it? Don't tell me someone tried to steal my prize bulls?'

'No, it's nothing to do with you at all,' Davis assured him passively. 'As I promised, the railroad will have a man watching your shipment all the way to Cheyenne.'

'Whew! Had me worried for a minute there.'

'How about your ticket? You said you weren't sure how many would be travelling.'

'Yes, I didn't know if another man or two would join me and the family. Turns out, it's only the six of us.'

'OK, that's you, your wife and your four children?'

'That's right.' Sketcher shook his head. Then making idle conversation the policeman would overhear, he added: 'And it's the last time the kids will make the trip with me. After the excitement from the first auction was over, the lot of them were bored to tears. I couldn't even take the wife with me after the first day.'

'I know how that is.' Davis sympathized. 'My three kids get rowdy after church service every week. Can't coop the youngster's up − got too much energy.'

'My wife claims the kids siphon off what energy we have. It gives them more and leaves us drained.'

He laughed, all the while making out the required tickets.

'What's your name, fellow?' the cop butted in.

'Sidney Grey,' he replied. 'Were you looking for me?'

His bushy eyebrows lifted, 'Why would I be looking for you?'

Sketcher shrugged. 'I thought maybe there had been a wire sent from Wyoming. A close friend of the family was shot a few days ago. I thought maybe some news arrived, after I had checked out from the hotel.'

'I ain't in the habit of runnin' errands for the telegraph company.'

'My mistake,' Sketcher apologized, 'but you did ask for my name.'

'And you have a wife and kids?'

'Yes, my wife is getting settled in the family car. With four kids, it's a real chore to travel. Take my advice, sir. Don't ever take your children on a long train ride.'

Rather than reply, the cop spun about and lumbered off.

'What's his problem?' Sketcher asked the agent. 'Someone steal his wife?'

Davis looked around, as if making certain no one was listening in, then leaned forward. 'One of their fellow officers was found dead in a back alley. They are looking for a street woman who might know something about it.'

Sketcher whistled under his breath. 'From the number of policemen around, she wouldn't stand much chance of getting on the train.'

'They'll find her,' the agent proclaimed. 'The Irish are a tough bunch — have to be, to control the streets of Chicago.'

Sketcher said: 'Glad they aren't looking for me.'

Davis passed him the train tickets and offered a professional smile. 'Good to have you travelling with us, Mr Grey. Maybe we'll see you again for next year's auction.'

'Could be,' Sketcher returned. 'But, as I told the policeman, I won't be bringing the family. Too much work.'

'I hear you,' Davis said. 'Have a good journey home.'

Sketcher boarded the family car and walked down to join Pamela and the children. He and the woman both uttered a collective sigh as the train pulled out of the station.

'Well, Mrs Grey,' Sketcher remarked, 'You are on your way to a new home.'

Pamela smiled — a most charming simper — and placed her hand over his own. 'I thank God for having you come into our lives. I don't think we could have survived another winter in that burrow, not with Officer McGowan's friends looking for us. . . .'

'Not a pleasant thought,' Sketcher agreed.

'But what about our new living arrangements?' she asked. 'You never did explain what kind of housing we could expect.'

'You've got a thousand dollars,' he said. 'You can do and have whatever you want.'

'Oh, no,' she said sternly. 'The cost of the kids staying at your hotel, the baths, the new clothing and shoes this morning, the train tickets – all of that has to come out of the reward money.'

He chuckled. 'If you say so.'

'And what am I expected to do in the town of Valeron? Didn't you say it was quite small?'

'It has all of the usual stores, a hotel, bakery, even a sheriff's office with a jail. There are quite a few farmers and some other ranchers nearby. We've a stage and express office that handles the telegraph and mail, same as a bigger city.'

'You said there was a school for the children?'

'Uh, not exactly a school. The three Valeron mothers and another gal or two do the teaching out at the ranch. A few locals send their kids out there to learn their lessons.'

'Then the Valeron ranch is separate from the town of Valeron,' she concluded.

'And you can stay at whichever you prefer.'

'If I were your actual wife, then I would stay at the ranch.'

'Yes. I would have a house-raising party and a dozen men would pitch in and construct a six- or seven-room house. Probably wouldn't take but a couple weeks.'

Pamela had been watching him intently, but she suddenly lowered both her gaze and her voice.

'Would you want that? I mean, a wife and four kids?'

Sketcher cursed his procrastination. 'I've been trying to find the courage to suggest that might be an option,' he told her carefully. 'But I don't want you feeling obligated. What I did for you, I'd have done for anyone – even had it been a man and wife with children. You're not indebted to me.'

She lifted her eyes – the dark chocolate spheres glistening in the early afternoon light. 'Sketcher, I allowed you to hold me close and kiss me. That wasn't only for comfort or compassion. I wanted to feel your arms around me, to feel as if you cared.'

'I do care!' he replied adamantly. 'You're the most wonderful girl I ever met. And the children – I've grown very fond of them all. I would give anything to have you as my wife and to love our four kids as their father.'

Another smile came to Pamela's lips, but it was more than a show of affection, it was an enticement, a beckoning.

Sketcher leaned over and kissed her. She kissed him in return and he knew there would be no searching for love in his life ever again. With a wonderful woman and four children, he was going to be a family man.

CHAPTER TEN

Jared wasted no time. He began visiting the store owners and everyone else in town, while he sent Shane and Doggie to all of the outlying ranches and mines – all except for Strang's place. He would let them find out about the new laws he was implementing in Solitary on their own.

The King High saloon was the one place he thought he might encounter trouble. Rex Frenner was the owner. He had no fewer than a dozen men with guns on his payroll, which made sense as he acted as the town's only banker. He didn't loan money or pay interest – just the opposite, in fact. The local proprietors all paid him a fee to protect their money or valuables.

Not a domineering-looking man, Rex was a little taller than average height, and carried some extra bulk around his middle. Obviously, he enjoyed his prosperity. He bid Jared take a seat in his office and sat behind an expensive polished oak desk.

'You're Wyatt Valeron's what? Brother?'

'Cousin,' Jared replied. 'And I'm going to find out who the second shooter was that nearly killed him.'

'I heard about the gunfight.'

'Hardly a fair contest,' Jared objected. 'One man holding a gun on him and another hiding in the darkness ready to shoot. If Wyatt wasn't the fastest man alive with a gun, he would have had a bullet through his heart and another through his brain.'

Rex showed no surprise. 'I only heard there had been a shootout, but that sounds more like Gino's style.'

'Gino, the range detective that took him on?'

He harrumphed. 'Back-shooters shouldn't try facing a man, they don't have the sand for it.'

'You knew him?'

'Heard a few stories about him, and he gambled in my casino a little. Gino was the kind of range detective who gives any of the honest ones a bad name. He was known to have eliminated men that were supposed rustlers.' Rex grunted his contempt. 'More often than not, he was getting rid of someone's competition, rather than an actual thief or rustler. Gino is the man you hired to kill a rival or an enemy. He had no conscience or scruples.'

'A loner, was he?'

Rex gave a bob of his head. 'Never seen him keep company with anyone else. He was the lowest order of human being.'

'I don't suppose you have heard anything about who the second shooter might have been?'

The man lifted a hand in a negative gesture. 'I haven't taken an interest in the shooting, but I might know who to talk to.'

'You are the town leader,' Jared proposed. 'Would you consider becoming mayor?'

Rex blinked in surprise. 'I run a saloon and casino,

son. Why would I want a position like that?'

'Because you have the respect of the rest of the people in town. Because I need someone to back up the rules I want to put in place.'

'What sort of rules?'

'I'm going to enforce a new gun law in town – no one carries a sidearm unless cleared by me or one of my deputies. Also, anyone who causes injury or damage will have to pay for it – either in cash or cleaning up after the horses for a set length of time. The signs are being posted around town and I've got four or five men who will enforce it.'

'What about my guards?'

'They are for security's sake,' Jared approved. 'Only rule for them is to not wear their guns outside in the street. In your place is fine.'

'I see where this is headed. The power of the Valeron family meets the might of the Strang family.' He chuckled. 'Could be an all-out war.'

'If Strang pushes it, the war will be short . . . and he will lose.'

'You sound pretty confident,' Rex admitted, 'but so was Wyatt.'

'Wyatt believes in fair play. He's a law-abiding town tamer.' With a crooked grin, 'For myself, I believe in only one thing: if forced to fight, you fight to win, and you win however you can. I'll do whatever I have to do, Mr Frenner, to get justice for my cousin. The yellow snake who hid in the shadows is going to be punished. That's what I intend to do, punish the guilty.'

'You're wearing a badge.'

Jared remained steadfast. 'I will do this within the

bounds of the law, or I'll do it in spite of the law. Like I said, in a fight, I do whatever is needed to win.'

'What exactly do you want from me?'

'Only what I outlined. Be proclaimed as town mayor and support the gun ordinance. As for your men, have them leave their guns here at the saloon any time they leave the premises. I don't want any chance of gunplay on the streets.'

'I suppose it is time we attempted to civilize the nearby ranchers and miners,' Rex said. 'There's been too much violence lately.'

'Then you'll do it?' Jared queried.

'I'll accept the mayor's job and give the order to my men. Does that suit you?'

'Yes.' Then Jared added hopefully, 'Plus, I would appreciate any information on that second shooter. If you hear something. . . .'

Rex knew that was the end of the request. He rose up and stretched out his hand. As Jared took it in a handshake, the saloon owner tipped his head slightly forward. 'I'll see what I can do.'

Brett was visiting with Wendy when the town runner brought a telegram. He reached out to receive the cable, but the boy handed it to Wendy.

'It's from Sketcher,' the youth announced. 'He's on his way back from Chicago.'

Wendy dug out a coin for the boy and unfolded the piece of paper. 'It's addressed to me, but it is intended for Dad.'

Brett frowned at his sister. 'Why you first? That makes no sense.'

'Neither does the message,' she said. 'Listen to this. Sketcher is asking me to have July go to the ranch and pick up the three-seat Surrey, the one the ladies use when they go shopping or for family events. He wants him and a couple of cow hands to meet him in Cheyenne.'

'The cow hands is expected,' Brett said, then curiously lifted his shoulders. 'What's Sketcher thinking about with that oversized buggy? Is he going to transport the Hereford bulls home in luxury and comfort?'

July grinned. 'Now there's something I'd pay to see – sticking a couple bulls in one of them carriages.'

Wendy laughed at their jests. 'I can't imagine what he has in mind, but you'd better round up a horse, July. You can take this message to Dad and bring back the carriage. The timetable says Sketcher won't reach Cheyenne for another couple days.'

'Right,' July was eager to comply. 'We can house the Surrey in the barn until time for me to leave for Cheyenne.'

'Make sure you get a couple of good hands for bringing those bulls home,' Brett added to his list of things to do. 'Have Reese line out the help. He'll make sure they can handle cattle and themselves. I'd wager most of those Hereford bulls cost near or over a thousand dollars each. Don't want to risk that kind of investment.'

July showed a wide grin. 'By Hannah! If I die, I want to come back as a Hereford bull. A hundred to one odds with all those heifers. What a life, huh?'

Wendy was not amused. 'Careful what you wish for. I can make the first half of that wish come true.'

July sobered. 'No, Miss Wendy! I'd sure hate to die before my time. And, as long as you're still on this here

121

earth, I'll be forever proud to just hold your hand.'

Brett shook his head in dismay. 'Never have I seen a bull change into a steer so quick.'

Remmy entered with Wyatt's lunch. He had recovered to the point where he could move enough to sit up and scoot back to use the pillow and headboard for support. He did not miss the girl's worried expression as she came forward to place the wooden tray on his lap. He waited until she sat down next to the bed to ask the obvious question.

'So, what did my cousin do?'

'There is now a law against anyone carrying a firearm on the streets of Solitary. Guns are to be checked at the old trading post before entering town to shop, gamble, drink or visit. Your pals Landau and Doggie are wearing badges. Cliff is in charge of the guns.'

'Good thinking,' Wyatt condoned the action. 'It will keep the innocent people out of harm's way.'

'Rex Frenner has taken on the role of mayor,' she continued with the news. 'He has come out in support of the new ordinance.'

'Jerry is using his head,' Wyatt praised his cousin. 'Sounds like everything is well in hand.'

'*Well in hand*!' Remmy cried. 'The Strang bunch will never give up their weapons! There's going to be a battle when they come to town.'

Wyatt smiled at her concern. 'Jared won't let that happen. If there is a fight, he will take it to the Strangs . . . and they will be durned sorry for crossing him.'

'Yes, but . . .'

Wyatt lifted his hand to silence her protest. 'Jared is a

hunter, Remmy. It's what he loves, and he does it better than any man I've ever met. He can slip up on a buck like a gentle breeze. He's a ghost in the woods or at night. Jerry once got back one of his favourite horses that had been taken by a band of renegade Indians. He followed them for 20 miles and retrieved the horse without waking or harming a single Indian. Takoda and Chayton call him White Wolf because of his prowess.'

'Ed Strang will not be caught sleeping.'

'So much the worse for him and his boys.'

Remmy remained quiet until Wyatt finished his meal. Then she retrieved the tray and leaned over to kiss him. The endearment was something she had started doing each time she left the room.

'If I'd have known I would get such warm and special treatment for a simple gunshot wound, I would be looking for someone to shoot me every time I get on my feet.'

She smiled. 'I'm responsible for this wound. I don't give away that kind of affection to anyone else.'

'You're a fine woman, Remmy,' he praised her. 'If I was to ever look for a lifelong mate, you would be the first stop on my list.'

She cocked an eyebrow. 'Just how long is your list?'

Wyatt chuckled. 'Actually, your name is the only one I can think of at the moment.'

'I'm legally dead. Does that make a difference?'

'Man takes what he can get in this part of the country. You're sure enough the prettiest dead person I ever laid eyes on.'

She laughed. 'What a charmer you can be, Wyatt.' And she left with the empty dishes and tray.

Wyatt stared at the door after she had gone. The yearning was there, to belong to someone, to have the love of a good woman. After this battle was over and done with, he wondered if he might consider a change in his lifestyle.

Strang's foreman was August Newman, a cattleman with twenty years' experience. Jared and Shane caught up with him as he had about a dozen riders hazing a herd away from a valley that had some fine grazing pastures.

August had two men at his side, but neither was armed. The foreman didn't pack a gun, other than for a rifle in a scabbard, secured to the saddle. He was weathered, looked capable, and his cheek bulged from a large chew of tobacco.

'How-do!' Jared greeted the three. He then directed his attention to the elder of the trio. 'I'd reckon you are the Strang ranch ramrod – August Newman?'

'I go by Gus,' the foreman replied. 'And I 'spect you're a couple of Valeron strays.'

'Jared and Shane,' Jared confirmed. 'I see you're busy protecting the winter feed.'

'Ain't been a lot of rain this summer,' Gus said. 'Be a long winter afore we will see green grass again. Being from a ranch of your own, I reckon you know we got to preserve enough fodder to get the cattle to that first spring rain.'

Jared hooked his leg over the pommel of the saddle, as relaxed as if he was sitting next to a campfire and about to read a book. Gus recognized this was a congenial meeting and waved the other two men back to work. Once they had ridden off, he spat a stream of tobacco into the dust.

'Reckon you tracked me down for a reason. Say what you came to say, Valeron.'

'You probably heard about my cousin being ambushed in town.'

'Word is, it was a straight-up gunfight.'

Jared snickered at the false report. 'I wouldn't call having the drop on a man a straight-up fight. Gino had his gun aimed at Wyatt, while my cousin's gun was still in its holster.'

Gus processed the news and a wrinkle creased his brow. 'That don't surprise me none. Gino was a known back-shooter. It's a wonder he dared face your cousin at all.'

'He didn't do it alone,' Jared informed him. 'He had a rifleman backing his play – hidden in the shadows.'

'No one said anything about a second shooter.'

Shane spoke up. 'Few men would brag about a set-up like that. One man holding a gun on Wyatt, while the other had his rifle aimed and ready to fire.'

Gus altered his chaw from one side of his mouth to the other. 'This Wyatt must be one lucky son to have survived a set-up like that.'

'He was hit in the chest when he downed Gino,' Jared explained. 'The man with the rifle was off-line an inch or two and creased Wyatt's skull.' Jared eyed the man with a steady peruse. 'That second shooter is guilty of attempted murder.'

Gus kept a poker face. 'And who do you suspect was behind that there rifle?'

'You know Ed and his boys, Gus,' Jared put the question to him. 'All four of the Strang brothers were inside Maxine's place at the time of the attack. I've had a gent or two tell me the older Strang sons are good boys.'

'Jack and Carver ain't no troublemakers,' the ramrod endorsed the pair. 'If they were inside the parlour, they were riding herd on Hud and Aldo.'

'As it couldn't have been one of the boys, who would you point a finger at?'

Gus spat into the dust again. 'You're flippin' cards, trying to land one in the hat, but I ain't gonna make a guess. Besides which, it don't sound like you can prove anything.'

'We come from a big ranch, too,' Shane chipped in. 'Jared's brother is the overall foreman. There sure isn't much he doesn't know about what goes on with the men. If one of them causes trouble, he knows who to talk to in order to straighten it out.'

Jared took over again. 'I don't expect you to oppose your boss, but we don't want this to escalate into a fight that will get a lot of good men killed. We're looking for one man who is guilty of attempted murder; plus Aldo and Hud are guilty of beating Maxine's bouncer to death, and the pair also killed a gambler a while back. All the bouncer did is try to stop them from knocking around one of the parlour girls, and they kicked him to death. The story on the gambler is that he won too much of the boys' money and they made him pay with his life. I'm asking you to take a stand, to keep the hired cow punchers from getting involved.'

Gus frowned. 'I played cards a time or two with that gambler fellow. He was one of the few card-slingers I ever met who didn't cheat.'

Jared made a second plea. 'We don't want to hurt anyone who is merely riding for the brand. This isn't a dispute between two ranches, a ranch and farmers, or even sheep. This is a couple of ornery sons from one family who have no respect for other people's lives, and the craven bushwhacker who didn't have the guts to show himself.'

Gus paused to spit again. 'All I can tell you is that Jack and Carver are good boys. Those two and the old man are often at odds about Hud and Aldo. Them are the ones who are loco wild.'

'Let's hope Jack and Carver stay out of any fight.'

Gus wiped his mouth with the back of his hand. 'So what is it you're asking of me? Make it plain, so there's no misunderstanding.'

'When I come to arrest Ed and his two killer sons,' Jared said unwaveringly, 'I don't want to have to worry about wounding or killing a bunch of innocent men, including your riders . . . or maybe you. I'm only after the guilty party.'

'I've worked for Ed for the past five years. I come over when my own little ranch went broke. He pays decent wages and allows me a free hand to take care of his cattle.'

'That tells me you are an honourable, hard-working sort,' Jared said. 'And I'll say this again – we have no wish to hurt or fight with anyone not involved in these crimes. However . . .' Jared's voice turned cold as ice, and he bore into the man with a deadly gaze, 'I will do whatever it takes to bring those three men to justice – Hud and Aldo, plus whoever shot Wyatt. If that means killing a dozen of your men, if it means killing you and every horse, cow or dog on the place, I'll damn well get the job done!'

Gus appeared to swallow his chew. It took a moment before he could clear his throat. 'I hear you posted one of them there ordinances agin' carrying a gun in town.'

'It's to make a point – I don't want any shooting where a bunch of bystanders might get hurt or killed during this little fracas.'

Gus exhaled and bobbed his head. 'All right, Valeron. I'll do what I can to keep my boys from joining in the fight agin' you. That good enough?'

Jared relaxed, swung his leg back down and found the stirrup with his foot. 'Remember, Gus, when this is over, the Strang family – whoever is left standing – will still need a foreman.'

'So long, Valeron,' he said gruffly. 'Good luck finding that second shooter.'

CHAPTER ELEVEN

Remmy looked much better. The area around her one eye was still discoloured, but the swelling had pretty much disappeared. Her lip was back to normal, with only a crooked line remaining where it had been split open. She was seated next to Wyatt on the back porch. A row of chairs and a couple of small tables had been placed there for getting air and enjoying the shade in the afternoons or early evening.

Jared walked over and took the chair next to Wyatt.

'What mischief have you been up to, cuz?' Wyatt asked. 'There's a good many rumours flying about.'

'Any odds being given at the King's High?'

Wyatt chuckled. 'I don't know. If they start betting against you, how much can you afford to wager?'

Jared grinned. 'Bet the house, partner. We've got all the aces.'

'Always did admire your confidence.'

'Something the two of us shared . . . until you let some lowlife, range-snoop put you down.'

'The man had a gun pointed at him!' Remmy argued for Wyatt from his other side. 'And there was a second shooter hiding in the dark! He's darn lucky to be alive!'

Both Valerons laughed at her coming to Wyatt's defence. The reaction caused Remmy to swat Wyatt on the arm.

'It's not funny!' she cried. 'You got yourself in a position where you had no chance at all.'

'We were laughing at you, not at the gunfight,' Jared explained, still grinning. 'Wyatt never needed anyone to stand up for him before. It just sounded funny.'

Remmy glared at Wyatt. 'You're laughing at me because I care?'

'Never!' Wyatt yelped like stepped on dog. 'It was Jer . . . I mean, the fact he was laughing. I would never laugh at you – not when you're being serious!'

Jared could not prevent a second round of laughter, this time at Wyatt's lame reply. He was nearly folding at the middle with mirth.

Remmy stood up and shook her finger in Wyatt's face. 'If you want your supper, you can darn well get it yourself!'

Then she stomped back into the main building.

'Thanks a heap, Jer,' Wyatt complained. 'Now I've got the best servant a man ever had mad at me.'

'Time you were doing for yourself, cuz. Dad-gum! Next thing you know, that gal will have you eating out of her hand. If you remember not so long ago, we shared a vow to be the last of the never-say-marriage bachelors.'

Wyatt displayed something Jared had never before seen – he blushed with embarrassment. The shock of his reaction caused Jared to jump to his feet.

'What!' Jared barked the word sharply. 'You don't mean that you're . . .' He struggled to find the word he wanted. 'You're not saying you. . . .' But he still could not complete the sentence.

'Jerry,' Wyatt said carefully. 'I haven't made a decision yet.' He shook his head slowly back and forth. 'It's just that, well, Remmy is too good for this kind of life. And I . . .'

'And you're gonna ask her to run away with you!' he challenged. 'Think about what that means, Wyatt! Remmy doesn't pack a gun. She can't back your play when you start cleaning up a town or running down a pack of killers. What kind of life are you talking about?'

A pained and confused look was etched into his face. 'I don't know,' he muttered softly. 'It's what I'm trying to say. I want . . .' He sighed. 'Hell, Jer! I don't know what I want . . . other than her.'

Jared eased back into his chair. 'Never thought it would happen to you, cuz, and that's the gospel truth.'

'Me neither,' Wyatt groaned. 'She slipped inside my defences and took me by surprise. I didn't see it coming.'

'Like the shot from that second shooter,' Jared grumbled. 'Only twice as deadly.'

'Exactly,' Wyatt agreed. 'She is such an angel, with the sweetest lips I ever tasted, and her heart is as pure as a baby's.'

'Holy ham-hocks!' Jared whined. 'I never thought I'd ever hear you say something so sugary and sappy. She got to you good.'

'Like trying to fight off cholera or smallpox,' Wyatt went on. 'She infected my heart and brain. I can't think of anything but her.'

Jared heaved a sigh and reached over to pat Wyatt on the arm. 'It happens to the best of men, cuz. I gotta say, I never figured it would happen to one of us.'

'I feel like I'm letting you down.'

Jared cleared his throat. 'I told Shane about that girl, way back when. The one I lost my own heart to.'

'Oh,' Wyatt said with some excitement. 'I was going to tell you next time we got together. I spotted your sweetheart a short while back. She still lives in Cheyenne.'

'Yeah?' Jared perked up at the news. 'How'd she look?'

Wyatt made a face. 'Like a watermelon with legs.' At his cousin's look of surprise, he turned his head from side to side. 'She had two children tugging on her skirt and looked as if she might have eaten one of her young to cut down on mouths to feed.'

'Damn, Wyatt!' Jared charged. 'Couldn't you put a little of that sugar you were spreading around about Remmy on the news you're giving me?'

'Looked as if she'd been eating way too much sugar . . . and anything else that wasn't fast enough to outrun her.'

Jared wrinkled his brow thoughtfully. 'She did have a rather full figure for a gal of fifteen,' he recalled. 'And, now that you mention it, her ma was a pretty large woman.'

'Look at the mother if you want to see what the daughter will look like,' Wyatt philosophized.

'Her pa wasn't all that big.'

'He was probably working sixteen-hour days back then. He's packed on quite a bit of table-muscle since then, too. I reckon he could eat a fair-sized hog and lick his fingers for more.'

Jared uttered a mild profanity. 'Now look what you've done, Wyatt! I don't even have a girl to dream about any more.'

'On the contrary, there's a lot more of her to dream about.'

'Oh, thanks a bunch. I come all the way to this one-out-house town to even the score for you, and what do I get for all my trouble? Crushed dreams about my girl and I've lost my one, solid bachelor-at-arms.'

'Maybe we should stick to the chore ahead, Jer. You're tying up a lot of hired help from the ranch. Have you got a plan yet?'

'Our new mayor convinced a gent to come forward about the second shooter,' Jared told Wyatt. 'He stated that he saw Ed Strang light out like his pants were afire a few seconds after you were shot full of holes. He claimed Ed was riding with a rifle across his lap. Can't be much doubt about him being the shooter.'

'Knowing Ed's our man, what're you going to do?'

'I'm gonna arrest Ed and two of his sons.'

'Didn't you tell me they were fortifying the ranch?'

Jared bobbed his head affirmatively. 'That's what Takoda says. He and Chayton are keeping an eye on things out that-away. He counted ten men constructing defensive positions and a couple of scouts keeping watch.'

'Preparing for a war.'

Jared grinned. 'Not the kind of war we're bringing 'um. They are in way over their heads.'

'Wish I could be there to see it.' Wyatt expelled a deep breath. 'But Remmy would scald my hide for even suggesting it.'

'See? What'd I tell you?' Jared scoffed. 'You're hen-pecked already . . . and you ain't even hitched yet!'

CHAPTER TWELVE

Sketcher stepped onto the platform and met up with Locke and July. After greeting them, he also bid howdy to the two ranch hands who had come along. Amos and Johnson were both men he had worked with for the last two or three years. Knowing they were capable men, he led them to the cattle car and had them take charge of the six bulls.

Locke had followed along silently, waiting until Sketcher finished with the Herefords. His patience came to an end once the bulls were moved to the holding pen.

'Now, Sketcher,' he began the inquisition. 'Suppose you fill me in. Why the need for the Surrey? What are you intending to haul in a three-seat carriage?'

Sketcher took on a rather sheepish countenance. 'If you'll come with me to pick up my luggage, I'll show you.'

'Did you draw so many sketches that you need a wagon to haul them all?' July asked, walking alongside of the two men. 'I mean, why else would you . . .' but he stopped talking.

A comely young woman and four little kids, ranging from four to eight years of age, were all standing on the

134

dock. Each and every one clean, neatly dressed, and smiling broadly at Sketcher. He walked forward to join them and turned around to face Locke and July.

'This is Pamela,' he introduced the woman, then began to point at each child. 'These two older kids are Monte and Tess. The other two are David and his little sister, Annie.' Taking a deep breath, he finished: 'Mr Locke . . . July . . . meet my new family.'

Locke sputtered, totally flummoxed. 'The family!' His voice squeaked uncharacteristically. 'Sketcher, you mean this young lady and these children? You're taking them on as *your* family? All of them?'

'Reckon so, Mr Valeron. That is, soon as we visit a Justice of the Peace.' He directed his words at both men. 'I was hoping you would stand up with me, July. And I'd be right proud if you, Mr Valeron, would do me the honour of standing with my bride.'

July whistled his amazement. 'Talk about the short way to fill an empty home. This is really something!'

'They were street urchins,' Pamela explained the children's unfortunate station at this point in their lives. 'Abandoned and orphaned. I took them in to keep them from starving. Sketch and I met and got to know each other and . . .' She displayed a pixie-simper. 'We agreed we should raise them as our own.'

Locke swung his gaze back to Sketcher to see his nod of accord. Convinced of the man's sincerity, he swallowed his amazement and stepped forward. Taking hold of Pamela's hand, he offered her his best smile.

'You've chosen a fine man, young lady,' he said with a welcoming smile. 'It will be my pleasure to stand at your side as a witness or whatever is needed at the proceedings.'

'Thank you,' she said politely. 'And the children thank you, too.'

'Looks like we're gonna have to build another bunkhouse to handle this new family,' July remarked. 'They sure aren't gonna fit into Sketcher's living quarters. That's what – a two-room cabin?'

Locke dismissed the trifle. 'I'm sure there's a story that goes along with this wedding, but let's not press for any further explanation right now. We need to get this ceremony and paperwork attended to as quickly as possible. It's a full day's ride to the ranch, especially with six bulls in tow.'

'Shouldn't take but a few minutes to make us a legal and binding family,' Sketcher said. 'Not with you vouching for me.'

'July,' Locke spoke to him, 'Tell Amos to get the bulls moving. We'll catch up with him and Johnson down the road.'

'I'll get them started, Mr Valeron,' July accepted the order. 'I'll see you over at the Justice of the Peace's office.'

Jared and Doggie were on the street when Jack Strang rode into town. He had a couple of riders with him, but none of the three were packing a gun. Spotting the badges on the two men's vests, the three turned their mounts towards them.

'You must be Valeron,' Jack said, as the three men stopped their horses. He stared at the glinting piece of metal. 'Is that a Deputy Marshal badge?'

Jared grinned. 'Deputy United States Marshal,' he corrected. 'Doggie here tells me you are the intelligent, level-headed member of the Strang family. Good to finally meet you . . . Jack Strang is it?'

The gent gave a bob of his head. 'I'm glad to hear Wyatt Valeron is recovering. I reckon your deputy there has told you that me and my three brothers were inside Maxine's place when the showdown occurred.'

'A showdown usually means each side has an equal chance,' Jared pointed out. 'Holding a gun on a man while his own pistol is in its holster and having a second shooter hiding back in the shadows – that's a lowdown, cowardly ambush.'

Jack swallowed hard, not hiding his own dislike concerning the means of the attack. Still, he had come for a reason and he got to it.

'Mr Valeron,' he began. 'I'm here to ask if there isn't a peaceful way to settle this. Gino was a back-shooter and lower than scum at the bottom of a garbage bin. Wyatt killed him and did the entire country a favour. What is it going to take to satisfy you, while acting in your capacity as Marshal?'

'Three arrests will settle this without any further trouble from our side. I want your two brothers, Aldo and Hud, for the murder of Maxine's bouncer and the killing of an unarmed gambler a few weeks back. Along with those two, I want the man who pulled the trigger and tried to shoot my cousin through the head.' He watched for a reaction. 'That would be your father, Edmund Strang.'

Jack licked his lips, while not refuting the charge. 'Isn't there a compromise we can reach? Pa told me he gave Wyatt five-hundred dollars to pay for damages. The bouncer wasn't married, so his kin are likely satisfied. And the injured girl will end up with more money than she could make in several months.'

'How much did you pay the gambler's kin?'

Jack's shoulders sagged. 'He came around quite often, usually the first of the month after the miners and ranch hands got paid. No one I've talked to knows where he hailed from.' Then putting on a sincere expression. 'We will sure send off a couple hundred dollars if someone tracks down his folks.'

'How much are you going to give my cousin, for your pa trying to take his head off?'

'Name a price,' Jack said quickly.

'Now you sound like your old man,' Jared did not hide his distaste. 'Contrary to the mindset of nearly every rich person I ever met, money doesn't buy everything.'

Jack firmed his jaw and returned to sitting erect in the saddle. 'I'm trying to find some middle ground, Valeron. We don't want this turning into a bloody war.'

'Sorry, Jack,' Jared told him. 'Them are my terms: surrender your two brothers and your pa. As my cousin survived, I'm willing to turn this matter over to a judge. Had he died . . .' Jared uttered a snort of contempt. 'I would have killed each and every last one of you.'

Jack had made his offer and been slapped down. He did have family pride, albeit shaky from being on the wrong side of this affair. He regarded Jared with a hard stare.

'If you come to the ranch, you'll find a whole lot more guns against you than you can handle, Valeron. Better think about that.'

Jared ignored the threat. 'We Valerons and our hired hands don't worry much about the odds; we always get the job done. There's nine of us in town, more than enough to wipe your family and any help you might have right off the face of the earth.'

'I'm sorry we couldn't reach some kind of agreement.'

Jared studied the man. 'I won't like it if we have to kill you, Jack. You seem a decent sort.' Then with a sigh of regret, 'But we are going to arrest your brothers and your father. That's a promise.'

Jack lowered his head, trapped in a position he didn't want to be in. 'Come at us if you have to, Deputy. Just be forewarned, the number of guns and men, along with fighting from protective cover – it will all be on our side. You come at us and we will be forced to cut you down like a row of corn.'

'So long, Jack,' Jared said. 'Expect to see us real soon, and keep your head down when the shooting starts.'

Jack led his two men back the way they'd come. Doggie, who hadn't said a word, moved up to stand at Jared's side.

'Seems a decent sort.'

'We'll try it without any killing first,' Jared assured him. 'Jack is a man whose death I wouldn't like on my conscience.'

'What do I tell the guys?'

'Tomorrow,' Jared said. 'Ed will likely keep most of his men up all night worrying we might hit them after dark. Should make them only about half-alert by the time we arrive.'

'Hitting them tonight is what I would do,' Doggie agreed.

'Tell everyone to meet up at the trading post after supper,' Jared outlined. 'I believe I've figured out a plan that ought to work.'

139

'Brett won't like it if this ends up with a dozen dead bodies,' Doggie uttered a rare opinion.

Jared grinned. 'If things go as I expect, Brett will actually be proud of all of us.'

'Sounds . . . what's the word – optimistic?'

'Yep, that's the word,' Jared said. 'Have Takoda and Chayton find me. We won't be needing them at the meeting.'

'You aren't going to leave them out of the fun?'

'Just the opposite, Dog. I'm going to let them throw the first punch.'

'I'll spread the word,' Doggie said. 'Come daylight, everyone will be ready.'

CHAPTER THIRTEEN

Ed listened to Jack and grew red in the face. 'You were sent to make the guy mad! I want them to come out here in a rush, thinking they can run right over us. We have enough men to empty every one of their saddles before they know what hit them.'

Jack didn't agree. 'I hoped to avoid a lot of killing. That's why I didn't take a gun and had only the two horse wranglers go with me.'

'I reckon this new Valeron is as big a blowhard as the first. Probably told you how he could wipe us out single-handed.'

'Actually, he said there would be nine of them.'

Ed was taken aback at the news. 'Nine? That's one or two more than I would have thought.'

'Valeron seemed to think it would be sufficient . . . no matter how many guns we have in place.'

'How can he believe that? He saw a portion of our numbers when he talked to Gus.'

'I know, Pa. Gus told us both about his visit.' He put his hands on his hips. 'And Gus said he and several of the regular cow hands were not going to fight. Gus had played cards with the gambler Hud and Aldo killed. And a good many of the men admired Remmy. Them two couldn't have chosen a worse target for beating up one of Maxine's girls.'

'Bah!' Ed said in a huff. 'Our hired men will fight with us or else I'll send them packin' down the road!'

'There is an alternative to fighting, Pa. You three can give yourselves up without anyone being killed.'

'Do what?' Ed shrieked. 'Are you plumb loco?'

'Think about it, Pa,' Jack kept his voice calm, trying to reason with his father. 'You can claim you thought Wyatt saw you, which forced you to shoot him before he could kill you. I don't know, claim you were only there to see it was a fair fight or something. You can say you didn't know Gino wouldn't give him a chance. For a situation like that, the judge might only give you a few months – a year or two at the most.'

'And what about your brothers?'

'They were fighting with both men at the time they died. Easy to have an accidental death that way. They only have to claim they didn't intend to kill either of those men. It would draw them a manslaughter charge instead of two murder charges. I'd expect they would each get a couple years or so in prison.'

'You're mighty eager to hand out sentences, son.' Ed pinned him with a cool gaze. 'Are you a coward, or are you simply trying to take over the ranch in my place?'

'Damn it all, Pa!' Jack lost his poise. 'I'm trying to save all of our lives! The Valerons are experienced fighters. They have the US Marshal's office behind them. If we kill one of them, the army is going to show up on our doorstep. Are you ready to do battle with the army?'

'Enough!' Ed held up both hands to end the conversation. 'I want two riders keeping watch all night. As for the rest of us, the crew will sleep in shifts – half awake while the other half sleeps. If the Valerons try to slip in after dark, I want their hides peppered with lead!'

Jack heaved a sigh of defeat. 'Whatever you say, Pa.'

Pamela sat in the second seat of the carriage next to Sketcher. Annie was on the opposite side, having decided she wanted to sit close to her new father. The other three children were in the rear seat, chattering and pointing at the unfamiliar terrain. Having never seen a mountain or open plain, they took note of every bird, groundhog or chipmunk, and marvelled loudly when a group of antelope raced past their small caravan.

'It's all so different out here,' Pamela added her own amazement. 'I expected the sun, wind and openness, but this is such a drastic change from the city . . . it's going to take some getting used to.'

'We're almost to Valeron,' Sketcher told her.

'Another mile,' July contributed from his place up front driving the Surrey. 'You'll be able to see the town when we top this last hill.'

'And the name of the town is the same as the ranch?'

'Started out as a trading and shipping point, a central place for having stuff delivered or sent off to Cheyenne. However, with mining, farming, ranching, and our lumber business, the Valerons soon had a couple hundred people working for them. With such a great need for supplies and services, it was easier to build the stores than order everything from Denver or Cheyenne. Now there's a newspaper, barber and bath, bakery, and all the other stores a body needs.'

'And you are the foreman over the cattle?'

'I'm the second ramrod . . . so to speak. Reese Valeron is the general foreman and I basically oversee the cattle.'

'Will we have a real house?' Annie asked. 'Like the ones we seen from the train?'

'A real house,' Sketcher assured her. 'And you can have a dog and cat . . . even your own horse.'

Her eyes grew wide. 'Really? I can have a kitty?'

He laughed at how she chose to ask about the one thing she wanted most. 'Yeah, we keep cats around to control the mice. They can become a real nuisance if a person doesn't have a cat or two about.'

Pamela rested her hand on his. 'It's like a wonderful dream, Sketch,' she murmured, keeping her voice low enough that July wouldn't overhear. 'You are an answer to all of my prayers.'

He grinned at the remark. 'And you, my lovely wife, are an answer to a prayer I never expected to get.'

'That there's the truth,' July spoke up, having eavesdropped again. 'Sketcher and me both started out in the same way – all by our lonesome. Yet, here we are, both working for the Valerons. Now I'm courting about the prettiest gal in the country, and he's done got himself a bride who is also a rare beauty. Just goes to show how good fortune can smile on most anybody.'

'You know, July,' Sketcher complained. 'The only thing bigger than your ears is that mouth of yours.'

July laughed. 'Ain't it the truth.'

They had reached the crest of the hill and the town of

Valeron was spread out before them. 'We'll stop for a meal before continuing, July spoke again. 'Mr Valeron wants to have some time with his daughter, Wendy – she's my sweetheart,' he clarified. 'Wendy is the baby of Locke Valeron's family and he doesn't get to see her as often as he would like.'

'It's going to take a long time to learn all of the names and faces in the Valeron family,' Pamela declared. 'What if they don't like me?'

July dismissed the idea. 'A young, volunteer mother, with four kids in tow, married to a guy that everybody loves? No chance of that, Mrs Grey.'

'I could have answered that question myself, July,' Sketcher complained. 'How about, on the last leg of this journey, you stay in town with your sweetheart. I will do the driving and assure my own little wife how happy everyone will be to have her on the ranch.'

July laughed. 'Exactly what I had in mind, Sketcher. You've only had a coupla days on the train to get used to having a family. I reckon you would sure enough enjoy a little more time alone with them . . . before you get to your two-room hut and try to figure where everyone will sleep.'

'I swear, July,' Sketcher said, feigning anger. 'One of these days I'm gonna sketch a drawing of you with a busted nose!'

'Wow!' Monte spoke up from the back seat. 'Is that a real town? It looks so small.'

'It's nearly a mile away,' Sketcher told him. 'You can bet you'll find a few things you need – another set of clothes, some tasty pastries, a sugar stick for the ride to the ranch . . . everything you can think of.'

'Do I get a horse too, like you promised to Annie?'

'Yep. We'll build us a corral and have a half-dozen or so of our own. Maybe get us a milk cow, one you can milk morning and night. We'll also get some chickens so the girls can gather eggs.'

'Gee,' he said, the awe he felt evident in his voice. 'A real *home on the range* . . . just like a song I heard a couple of guys singing one time.'

'Don't forget the schooling,' Pamela spoke up. 'All of you kids are going to learn to read and write.'

'When we gonna have time for that?' Monte grumbled. 'With milking a cow, going hunting and fishing, taking care of a dog, riding a horse . . . I don't see how we can fit in going to school.'

'Man's got to get an education,' July jumped into the fray again. 'Need to be able to read a book and do your numbers. Man can't get by these days without having some book learning.'

'I don't see why,' Monte complained. 'Cows don't much care if you can read.'

'It's so you can get a job that uses your head and not just your back,' Sketcher told him. 'Look at July – he's being taught his trade by a girl.'

'No way!' Monte jeered.

'Yep,' July agreed. ' 'Cause she got an education in accounting, while I only learned enough to get by. A fellow needs to hold his head up, be able to read and write and talk proper. That's what it takes to get ahead, to get a job where you can earn a good living.'

'Finally,' Sketcher praised July. 'I suspected if you talked long enough, you would actually say something worth listening to.'

July laughed. 'It's a gift, Sketch, old son. If you would do a little more talking, you too might eventually say something worthwhile.'

'I'm anxious to meet this Wendy person,' Pamela quipped. 'I want to recommend she teach you something besides accounting . . . like manners!'

July looked over his shoulder at her, relieved when he saw she was teasing him. Even so, he reached up his free hand and tipped his hat.

'You have my humble apology for anything I might have said that was not to your liking, Mrs Grey.'

Sketcher laughed, as did Pamela. Then he smiled at her. 'See? You and the kids are going to fit right in.'

Remmy stayed out of the room while Wyatt was conferring with Jared. Once his cousin had left to meet with the other Valeron people, she approached his bedside and sat down in the chair Jared had been using.

'I didn't want to interrupt your war council,' she said. 'The way you two were whispering back and forth, one might assume you were planning a bank robbery or something.'

'Jerry and I have been in a few scrapes together,' Wyatt told her. 'He wanted me to hear his plan and approve of the action he is going to take.'

Remmy felt a pang of worry. 'It . . . it isn't going to mean a lot of killing, is it?'

Wyatt reached out and patted her knee. 'Jerry is known for having a temper and tackling any odds to get justice, but he's a thinking man, too. I'd say this was one of his better ideas – one that I'm guessing Brett would approve.'

'I remember you telling me about Jared's personal code of honour, one time when you were feeling rather melancholy.'

He smiled. 'All of the guys you've had to listen to since you came to Maxine's – I can't imagine how you recall the stories I've told you.'

'Every one,' Remmy avowed. 'Not because the stories are exciting and true, but because they are part of your life, your history.'

'You are part of my history too, Remmy,' Wyatt confided to her. 'More so than ever after taking care of me these past few days.'

'You also took care of me,' she reminded him. 'I was feeling about as low as my shoe-tops when you arrived in Solitary. I was in pain; I looked the worst I've ever looked in my life; and I was wishing I could die.'

'Remmy, I . . .'

She stopped his protest with a shake of her head. 'No, Wyatt,' she continued. 'I mean it. Do you have any idea how rotten my life is? I pick and choose my customers, but I still have to debase myself and allow men to . . . to. . . .'

He took hold of her hand. 'We are two of a kind, Remmy. I've been selling my gun, fighting other people's battles, sometimes killing a man simply because he was on the opposite side of those who hired me. The stories I've told you about Jerry and me, those are tales I can be truly proud of, because I didn't earn a dime helping him, I did it because my talent was needed and it was the right thing to do.'

'Maybe so, but you've saved lots of lives on your own, settling mining disputes, taming wild towns, and putting violent men behind bars. It's a job that someone had to do, and you are the most qualified man around.'

Rather than carry forward the subject, Wyatt gazed at Remmy and knew he couldn't let her continue to work and live in such a place.

'Valerie Remington,' he used her real name and squeezed her hand, 'you deserve so much more out of life. I'm little more than a good-for-nothing, slightly used and abused gunman, but I've some money put away. I'm of a mind to become a gunsmith. Would you consider moving to Valeron and helping me run my own store?'

Remmy studied him with a puzzled frown, as if unsure what his offer meant. Seeking clarification, she ventured: 'Are you asking me if I want to hire on as a clerk in your store?'

Wyatt grinned. 'I was thinking more of a partnership.'

A teasing smile played on her lips. 'Oh, so you want me to invest my own money in this store of yours. Is that is?'

Wyatt pulled on her hand until she was forced to lean over the bed. 'Not exactly the way I planned. It's more of a . . .' he sought the right word, '. . .intimate kind of part- nership,' he finished. 'One where a person needs a licence instead of a contract.'

Rather than continue playing games, Valerie lowered her head and placed a very generous, warm kiss on his lips. After a few seconds, she lifted her head and smiled down at him.

'Will that do for my answer?'

Ed was in a surly mood, grumbling through breakfast and stomping and snorting like a bull in cage. He shot a hard look at each of his four sons, then went over to the front window and jerked back the curtain so he could see the yard.

'Everyone awake?' He snapped off the words to Jack.

'We did like you said. Two riders were on patrol all night – still are – and the rest of the men slept in shifts. We had no less than six ready guns all night long.'

'Yeah,' Aldo whined, 'and we didn't see nuthen!'

'They're coming,' Ed vigorously maintained. 'They're coming today. We have to stay alert!'

'Five of us in the house,' Carver recounted for him. 'We've two in the shed, six on the perimeter and two on horseback scouting for signs.'

'Who's riding watch?'

'Sonny and Wade,' Carver spoke up. 'They were supposed to be back for breakfast at daylight.'

'So where are they?' Ed wanted to know.

'Sun is barely up,' Jack pointed out. 'They could be making a last sweep of the hills before coming in.'

The door opened and Sanders stuck his head inside. 'Looks like Wade and Sonny are headed this way,' he said. 'But something don't look right.'

Ed and all four boys went out onto the porch to have a look.

Two riders were indeed moving in the direction of the ranch house, but they looked stiff and odd sitting in their saddles. Both were completely erect and appeared to have their arms tightly pinned at their sides.

'What the devil?' Ed wondered aloud. 'It looks like they are guiding their horses with. . . .'

'The reins are between their teeth!' Jack exclaimed.

'Get them, Sanders!' Ed ordered.

Sanders and Cy had been doing the rotation with Wade

150

and Sonny. Both of them grabbed up their ready mounts and raced out to meet the two riders. When they reached them, Sanders began working on Wade, while Cy was busy with Sonny. Both men had been bound with rope!

All four horsemen returned to the front porch, climbed down from their mounts and secured the animals at the hitch rail. Before any of them could speak, Carver pointed up the hill.

'What's that?' he shouted. 'Looks like a wagon bed!'

'Boss!' Wade was the one to speak. 'Them fellers said to get everyone away from the tool shed.'

'Do what?'

'Yep,' Sonny joined in. 'Don't no men hide inside or stand anywhere near the shed.'

Ed threw his arms in the air. 'What the hell are you two blubbering about?'

Jack ignored the confusion and his father's questions. He yelled to the two men who had been using the small building for cover. When they appeared, he called them over to the house.

Even as they joined the group of men in front of the house, the wagon on the hill continued to draw closer. Now they realized several men were pushing the carry-all by hand. It continued to roll closer to the main house, until it was positioned less than a hundred yards away.

'What are they up to?' Carver asked Wade and Sonny. 'Is that all the message you brung us?'

Wade shrugged his shoulders. 'They said we were to all stay clear of the shed, that this was some kind of demonstration.'

'That's right,' Sonny agreed. 'Wade and me was both grabbed by Injuns. Then one of them Valeron boys told

151

us to tell you this here is an example of what you can expect, if you decide to fight.'

Ed swore vehemently. 'What to expect?' He watched as a man climbed into the bed of the wagon and threw aside a tarp. 'I sure ain't seen nothing that is going to—'

Then a Gatling gun opened up, firing rapidly, the rat-tat-tat-tat spewing bullets like a hailstorm. The men all ducked and a couple ran for cover, but the gun was not aimed at them. Each round slapped against the facing of the shed like the striking of a dozen hammers at one time. The savage pounding splintered off chunks of wood from the front wall and door of the shed, ripping it full of holes. No fewer than a hundred rounds shattered the door, tore through the interior and ventilated the entire structure.

Abruptly, the shooting stopped.

As a strange muteness greeted the early morning air, two dark shadows flew through the sky. The arc of their flight was exact enough to reach the shed. . . .

Twin explosions shattered the silence and blew the structure into a thousand pieces!

The shock of the blasts nearly knocked the men off their feet. Thunderstruck, covered in dust and splinters of wood, the men staggered about, coughing from the thick cloud and unable to see. The four horses, which had withstood the gunfire, jerked their reins loose from the hitch rail and bolted away.

As the smoke, ash, and dust cleared, a lone rider moved to within shouting distance.

'Ed Strang!' the man's voice carried an air of authority. 'I'm a deputy United States Marshal. You and your two sons – Aldo and Hud – are under arrest. If you resist, we will do to your house, barn and any other buildings still standing what we have done to the shed. You have two minutes to make up your minds.' He paused a few seconds, then added a final warning. 'Surrender to the law or be blown to hell!'

CHAPTER FOURTEEN

Ed tried to calm the room, but there was such ado and confusion no one voice could be heard. It took a full minute before Jack and Carver managed to silence everyone.

'We're out of this fight, Ed,' Wade told the old man. 'We didn't sign on to fight against that kind of fire power. If you want to fire us, go ahead. We're not going to be a part of this here skirmish!'

'It'd be suicide to stand against them!' Sonny agreed. 'Besides which, that's the law talking, a genuine US Marshal!'

'He's only a deputy,' Ed grumbled.

'Deputy or not,' Jack countered. 'They've got a gun that shoots a hundred rounds a minute, and a couple Indians who have demonstrated they can rain down on our positions with dynamite! We have no choice, Pa. We have to surrender!'

'You ain't the one going to jail, are you!' Ed exploded. 'Me and Hud and Aldo – we are the ones who will end up in prison!'

'For a couple years maybe,' Carver put in. 'Two or three years is better than dying.'

'If you're voting to fight,' Wade warned again, 'we are pulling out . . . me, Sonny and all the others. We was willing to stand at your side, even though we knew you were guilty. But not against a lawman, an RJ Gatling gun, and flying arrows carrying sticks of dynamite!'

'Remember my advice, Pa,' Jack pleaded with him. 'We will hire the best lawyer money can buy. He can maybe convince a judge that Hud and Aldo didn't mean to kill the bouncer or that gambler. And you thought Valeron was going to turn his gun on you – that's pretty much self-defence. None of the crimes are a hangin' offence. You only have to do a little jail time.'

Ed didn't want to listen. He searched for a way to fight back, a way to use his anger, the might of his men and guns. . . .

But reality and logic were too damning. Pitted against the rapid-fire gun, the explosives, and no fewer than nine armed men. Seasoned fighting men? Looking around him, he saw only defeat and fear. His loyal men, even his own sons, knew they had no chance against such long odds. He heaved a mighty sigh and raised his hand.

'No need losing all of our lives over this,' he spoke to Jack. 'You and Carver have been running the place for the last few years. And Gus is a good man to ramrod the crew. You can keep the ranch going while we're away.'

'Wait, Pa!' Hud cried. 'We can make a run for it!'

'Yeah,' Aldo joined in, 'we don't want to go to prison! We was just having some fun!'

'The only saddled horses have run off,' Wade spoke up.

'Me and the boys will be happy to drop our guns and walk away – whatever them Valerons demand.'

'Besides which,' Jack scolded his two youngest brothers, 'fun shouldn't mean killing people. A couple years in prison might force you to grow into men.'

'Your time is up!' came a shout from outside. 'What's it gonna be?'

Carver was nearest the door. He opened it and stepped out. 'Hold your fire!' he called to the Valerons. 'We accept your terms.'

Habitually falling into their old jobs with the army as ex-scouts, Takoda and Chayton were well out in front of the small procession on the ride home. Jared was between Landau and Shane on horseback, riding ahead of the buckboard Cliff was driving. After a time, Landau broke the silence.

'I've been trying to think of how I can break the news of this conflict to Scarlet,' he said, shaking his head. 'I come along on this campaign, expecting a kill-or-be-killed gunfight, with maybe a couple of us not returning home. Instead, the only two staying behind are taking over as lawmen for the town of Solitary. I'm gonna miss Doggie and Tiny.'

'Blew me away like a puff of smoke when they told me,' Jared summed up his own feelings. 'The new mayor is taking his job seriously and wants to make a real town out of the place. Tiny said he promised to pay them twice what they've been earning.'

'Must have liked the peace and quiet of law and order,' Shane chipped in. Then added: 'Not to mention he won't need near as many hired guns to protect his place.'

'Even so,' Jared observed. 'Those two sticking around took a distant second to learning Wyatt's decision.'

'Uncle Udal won't believe it,' Shane agreed. 'I remember him telling me once he expected Martin and Faro would be his only boys that would ever marry. Now Wendy has wired us that Sketcher showed up with the gal he met in Chicago and four kids. And danged if Wyatt isn't going to hang up his guns, get hitched, and open a business of his own.'

Landau grunted. 'Reckon the one due the biggest surprise will be Brett. He deputized Jared, thinking it would probably mean ending a dozen lives, and what happens? Jared ends up turning over the three guilty men to the US Marshals at Cheyenne without so much as firing a shot!'

'Worse for his reputation,' Shane sided with Landau, 'he didn't even hang the man who tried to kill Wyatt.'

'Guess I'm getting old,' Jared accepted the ribbing. 'Although I'd wager Ed and his two sons all get five years or more behind bars. I reckon that will have to serve as justice this time.'

'It's just as well,' Landau joked. 'I didn't see a single decent tree for a hanging anywhere.'

'Yeah,' Shane chuckled. 'And it's a lot of work to build a gallows. Right, Jer?'

'All funnin' aside,' Jared replied to Shane. 'If you go and find yourself a gal, I'll be the only bachelor in the family.'

'Cliff ain't tied the knot yet,' Shane pointed out, jerking his thumb back towards the wagon.

Jared grunted. 'It's not the same – like with Troy and Faro. They never ride with me when there's trouble or a problem to be solved with a gun. Besides, Cliff is already tied to the nanny's apron strings.'

Landau chuckled. 'I notice his daughter has taken to calling the girl Mommy, and I've not heard him correct her yet.'

'I suspect he's a goner,' Jared said, as if speaking of someone who died. 'Nope, it's down to me and Shane, because I know for a fact that Troy and Faro are both seeing gals.'

'Hate to bring this up, Jer,' Shane uttered the words with manifest reluctance, 'but I've been seeing one of the miners' daughters too. I gotta say she's about the sweetest girl I ever met.'

Jared stared at him with a horrified expression. 'Say it ain't so, cousin!'

Landau reached over and punched Jared on the shoulder. 'Don't worry, Jerry. If you get lonely for men like yourself, there's always the Indians, or you can visit Reb and Dodge, over where they are running Nash and his wife's ranch. Those two old-timers wouldn't mind the company.'

'Shucks. You could even head back to Solitary,' Shane chirped. 'Tiny and Dodge can line you up with one of Maxine's best girls.'

'I can't take a chance of that,' Jared retorted. 'Look what happened to Wyatt!'

Landau laughed. 'Sometimes love grabs hold of you, whether you want it to or not!'

'Gotta believe that,' Shane joined in. 'Take this thing with Sketcher – a wife and four kids and he's the same age as me!'

Jared sighed, 'I reckon it's the Valeron luck . . . even if Sketcher was never officially adopted. Him, Brett and

Wyatt . . . I never figured any of us would get married.'

'Well, as for me and most everyone else who knows you,' Landau said, grinning. 'We all believe you're a safe bet to remain a bachelor.'

'That's true,' Shane followed suit. 'No woman in her right mind would ever marry you.'

'Thanks a heap, fellows,' Jared quipped dryly. 'It's good to know my lot in life is secure.'